THE

OF

RUNES

by

Dagmara Drozdowska

Published by New Generation Publishing in 2020

First Edition

ISBN

Paperback	978-1-80031-855-7
Ebook	978-1-80031-854-0

www.newgeneration-publishing.com

New Generation Publishing

The Book Challenge

WHAT'S YOUR STORY?

This book was shortlisted in the Pen to Print Book Challenge Competition and has been produced by The London Borough of Barking and Dagenham Library Service - Pen to Print Creative Writing Programme. This is supported with National Portfolio Organisation funding from Arts Council, England.

Pen to Print

WHAT'S YOUR STORY?

Connect with Pen to Print
Email: pentoprint@lbbd.gov.uk
Web: pentoprint.org

Supported using public funding by ARTS COUNCIL ENGLAND

Barking & Dagenham

AUTHOR'S NOTES

Unlike original runic inscriptions, which were written in Old Norse, the runes used in this novel are to be translated straight into modern English.

Whilst Erica's story and Einarr's saga about the cursed rings are creations of the author's imagination, the symbols used in the novel are not. These are drawn from Viking culture and Norse mythology.

The fragment of the poem *Hávamál* (p.147), about the origin of the runes, is from a 13th century Icelandic manuscript. Of the many scholarly translations I examined, I chose to quote one by Carolyne Larrington, which you can find in 1999 Oxford World's Classics *The Poetic Edda* (ISBN 0-19-283946-2), as I feel this version conveys the poem's original intent as I imagine it.

Any similarity to names and/or events are coincidental.

For my parents. With love and gratitude.

Hi Carole and Peter!

Thank you so much for your support.

Enjoy the book!

x Daphneva

Prologue

London, 111 years ago

It was one of the hottest days in centuries. The sun looked down at the busy streets of London with not even one cloud keeping him company. Bells from a nearby church announced to the locals that it was already midday. The loud and dusty city centre was even more chaotic than usual. Horse-drawn carriages had to share the street with the packed omnibuses, leaving barely any space for pedestrians. Closing off most of the city centre made the surrounding streets very crowded indeed and the construction works were so loud that the nearby market sellers and the young boys selling newspapers had to work twice as hard to be heard.

'Extra! Extra! Today's big question! Will new London Underground be ever finished?'

A paper boy shouted to a dozen passers-by, waving a copy of the *Standard* like it was a sword. Another boy from a rival paper bellowed loudly, competing for attention:

'*Times* only! Early Edition! Interview with Mr Anderson! London Mayor!'

At that moment a person, looking very similar to the picture on the front page of the Times, stepped up to the red sign on the street. It read: *Warning! Men at Work. London Underground. Piccadilly Line. Do not Enter. Do not Commit a Nuisance.* The man disappeared behind the wooden gate.

'How is progress, gentlemen?' he said. Using one hand, he took off his top hat and greeted a standing nearby group of workers with a gesture. They looked at one another, unsure. It wasn't every day a toff like this would come down to the site. One of them, which looked like he could have been a foreman, stepped forward and started to say something:

'G'morning, sir. We weren't expecting you–'

'Interested in the progress, my man.' He gave the worker a broad smile. 'Could you direct me to – ah, never mind, there he is!'

The official made his way to the other side of a trench, careful to not dirty his shiny boots and very expensive suit. The person he'd spotted was hunched over in the shade, playing with his moustache and studying a map on a makeshift table. Even at this distance the archaeologist looked tall and distinguished. Not what most people might expect. Most people would think of archaeologists as earnest men with grey hair and hard hats, a trowel in one hand and a brush in the other.

The well to do walked over to him and said:

'You need to hurry up my friend. Her Majesty the Queen and the bugaboos in Westminster are starting to ask questions.'

The man looked up from his studying and blinked into the light of the day, the hand on his moustache paused in mid-fiddle. Mr Anderson, Mayor of London, continued, his tone sharp: 'It's taking too long, my brother. I don't know how much longer I can draw attention away.'

Straightening, the archaeologist placed his hands firmly on the table, covering the map. 'I know,' he answered tersely. 'I don't have much time either, but I'm telling you, we are very, very close!'

Mr Anderson looked unconvinced. The sunlight making his features hard.

'Look on the bright side,' the man chuckled. 'With thanks to us, Londoners will have more Piccadilly line than they ever thought possible!'

The joke, feeble as it was, withered under Mayor Anderson's stare.

'We are close! Soon! One more day! Does this sound familiar, Sir Roger? You said that twenty years ago!'

Sir Roger Wright bridged his fingers in front of his face and pursed his lips. Mr Anderson ignored him and continued:

'Did you consider, Sir Roger, that this might all be a myth created by the Scandinavians? That there is nothing down there, hmmm? Ye Gads man, we dug up nearly an entire city looking for it!'

Sir Roger smiled. It was a calm smile and belied nothing of what he was feeling at that moment. The delay weighed on him. It was taking its toll on his body as well as his spirit.

'Mayor Anderson,' he said. 'In just a few short months' time, my wife will give birth to a son. I know here–' he tapped his chest where his heart was '–that it will be a boy. I want him to be proud of his father.'

Sir Roger Wright knew that he was one of the greatest British archaeologists in history, in fact he had been knighted for his services. But even after all of this, he wanted to do more. To be remembered forever. He glanced down at the map.

'I want also to live long enough for my son to be able to meet his father,' he said.

'Soon, I will–'

There was a sudden commotion in the tunnel mouth. A workman who Sir Roger quickly identified as a man called George, scrambled the wooden scaffolding and rushed towards them. He stood, trying to catch his breath, wiping the sweat dripping from his forehead.

'Gentlemen,' he gasped, nodding to both, then turning his sight to Sir Roger, 'I think you would like to see this.'

The thing Sir Roger had been praying for decades was finally happening.

Without hesitation and asking no questions, he took off his coat and hat, rolled up the sleeves of his white shirt and looked at his watch. '*Finally,*' he thought. '*My dream is about to come true. At exactly 12:27, on this beautiful September day.*'

Following George, careful not to fall, he and the mayor disappeared below ground.

The workers at street level gathered around the trench. A crowd of Londoners behind the wooden fence was getting more curious by the minute.

'I bet they found a body,' said a burly man.

'Or treasure!' someone else guessed.

'Ere, treasure? What treasure?' said one of the newspaper boys.

'It'll be gold!' said a woman at the back.

'Nah, jewels,' said another.

'I thought they were building a railway?' said the friend of the first man in a curious tone.

'I'm telling you it's a body,' said his burly friend.

'Ere, let me see,' said the paper boy pushing forward.

An hour or so passed. By the time Sir Roger came back to the surface, half a dozen constables were trying to keep pedestrians from climbing over the barriers. A few members of the press had already been notified and gathered beside them. The air was hot and noisy, filled with speculation. As soon as everyone saw Sir Roger scramble up the trench, they fell silent. Expectant. One of the workers helped him up the last steps. He thanked him and wiped his hands on his thighs ready to face the crowd.

The archaeologist's shirt was not white anymore and his face no longer clean. Covered in dust and mud he looked like a golem. With a gesture of his hands, he asked everyone to step back. Then he grabbed a battered metal bucket lying nearby, tipped it over and stood on it.

'Ladies and gentlemen,' he began. 'I, Sir Roger Wright, am pleased to announce the greatest discovery in history!'

The crowd buzzed. Sir Roger continued:

'Down deep below the streets of our fine city, we have found a tomb.' He paused for effect. 'A tomb which I believe belongs to a Viking warrior named Einarr. And what I can tell you now is that Einarr was no simple warrior. He was a hero. Praised in the sagas of Norway, even today. And because of this, we can expect a great treasure to be buried with him.' The crowd buzzed even more.

'For now,' he continued, 'this place will be closed for everyone but our intrepid team of workers. However, everything we find – including any treasures –,' he said in a serious tone of voice, '– will be donated to the British Museum. As soon as we finish here, ladies and gentlemen, you will be able to see all the objects discovered today in their rightful place among history. I thank you.'

The press and crowd started to yell out their questions, but they were shouting to the air. Sir Roger had already disappeared underground again. What had seemed to be just another normal day in London when they'd woken up that morning, became one of the most important in the city's history.

Chapter 1

It was just after midnight.

A figure in a mask and hood stood in the middle of the Great Court at the British Museum. It was trying to work out about which way to go. The night outside was so foggy and cloudy that through the giant glass roof not even moonlight entered the hall. The figure was alone, here.

The building was monumental, and everything was surrounded by silence. Up until that moment, he'd had been feeling confident about what he had come to do. He was sure he would succeed. They'd been planning it for months. He and his boss. Except there he stood, the pitch black lit only by a torch, unsure about which staircase to choose. He had come to steal something very precious.

'It's this way…' said his voice muffled by the mask. The figure pointed his light onto the marble steps to the right. 'Or this? God, it looks too different in the dark.' The eyes of the figure blinked, trying to see the way to go. He pointed his torch at the staircase by the main entrance, the gesture brusque and frustrated.

The torch beam landed on the face of a chubby security guard, who squinted back at the blinding light.

'Hey!' the guard shouted. 'Who's there?' He pointed his light at the intruder and without hesitation started to run towards him. The masked figure flicked off his torch and took advantage of the darkness, running towards stairs in the middle of the Great Court. The guard darted forward. *Wow,* thought the intruder, *for such a fatty he's bloody fast*. He tried to make his way up the staircase. The marble steps were too slippery, and the figure fell.

'Hah! Got ya!' grunted the guard, as he managed to grab a hand. The intruder struggled as, panting, the guard scrambled for the walkie-talkie on his shoulder.

'I don't think so,' hissed the thief. He knew that the price to get caught was too great, so he started to fight full on. He tried to pull out of the guard's grip, wriggling and tugging. In the beam of his torch the guard caught a glimpse of bare forearm. A tattoo.

'Wait a minute,' said the guard. 'Have I seen this tattoo before?' He'd finally managed to grab the walkie-talkie with his free hand. He yanked the thief back toward him and spoke into shoulder. 'I need immediate backup in the Great Court,' he growled. 'I have an intruder in the museum.'

'Mike!' blurted the mysterious figure. So, he knew him, thought Mike. Did he indeed know him, too? 'Mike, listen, you don't understand,' the thief started to beg and strain against the grip as Mike the guard struggled to find his taser. He dropped it. This was the thief's chance and he took it. But Mike was onto him again. He felt a tug at his hood from the old guard. There was only one thing he could do. He pulled at the gun by his side.

'Will you just give it up, mate,' hissed Mike. He yanked the hood off the intruder and the mask came with it.

'You?' said Mike. Then he heard a gunshot. The old guard fell to the floor, wounded but still moving. The figure in the hood turned slowly and pulled the trigger once again, this time so precisely, that the guard had no chance.

The thief, angry and afraid, looked down at Mike the guard. He swallowed.

'No matter what,' he said to the cooling body, 'it wasn't supposed to go like this. You should have been on a break, your stupid fool.'

The guard's walkie-talkie crackled in the darkness like a death rattle. Reinforcements were coming. Re-masked and hooded, the figure ran fast through the dark empty museum halls, breathing loudly.

Fifteen seconds later, Mike's back-up guards appeared in the Great Court. They saw him in the sharp beams of their torches. They were too late.

Chapter 2

Erica Skyberg was on her way to work. She was smiling to herself because she knew one thing – it was Wednesday. For many people, Wednesdays were ordinary boring days, for her they were special. Wednesdays meant one thing – *he* will be there today. In the museum where she worked. In her department.

When she arrived at the Holmenkollen station, the blue line train going down to central Oslo, was already on the platform.

'Dørene Lukkes' – the Tannoy announced the closing door.

As much as most of the people would stand back and wait for another T-bane, Erica was not one of them. She ran quickly using her long legs and jumped in with her backpack missing by millimetres the closing door. And as much as she was quick, she was also clumsy. She immediately tripped over by her untied shoelace and all the books she was holding, toppled to the floor. Luckily for her it was too early in the morning and nobody else was on board. She gathered her things and found her favourite spot right by the window. She looked out at the entire city waking up.

Erica liked these morning journeys. The trains were still very empty, the streets were still quiet. She would pass by houses in the woods and watch their owners slowly getting ready to start their day. Yes, she liked this journey. At its beginning, the train is practically on top of the hill, so all the fjords are visible for miles. Erica Skyberg had lived in Holmenkollen with her grandmother ever since she could remember, but still the breathtaking view from up here, every single day brought joy in her heart. She took a deep breath in and a loud breath out and drifted away in her thoughts. The sun was just coming up above the water on this beautiful Wednesday morning, and she started to smile.

It happened a few weeks ago. All of a sudden, she noticed him. She noticed as well, that he came to see the exhibition every Wednesday, always at the same time, always with a drawing block and pencil. He just sat there for a good few hours, drawing one of the Viking ships. Erica liked Wednesdays. She would pass by him way too many times, just to catch his big blue eyes from behind his big round glasses. Just to see that smile. It was always definitely the most fleeting smile ever, and she could never tell if it was her or him who smiled first.

They had never exchanged more than a 'hi' or 'hello' but the butterflies in her stomach told her that she would love to be more than just a stranger to him. She felt a connection with him beyond the Viking ships and the shy smile. Even her friends saw it. But it was always the same, and hadn't she had a similar recent experience? She'd felt the same kind of amazing connection with that other guy not that long ago. However, it turned out it was all in her head. So, having this every Wednesday by the end of the day she was just a classic Erica: driving herself crazy with a million questions.

'Maybe he's gay? He definitely has a girlfriend. Guys like him are always taken. Then, *I like him, so knowing my luck he is in a relationship. Beside he doesn't show that much interest as well.* I mean –' Erica continued discussing this matter with herself, '– *if he were single and interested then he would ask me out, right? Because why not? Although he might be shy. Yes, that what probably what it is. He is shy!* Then: *No, he can't be. He's just not interested.'* Her train of thought stopped in its tracks as the announcement of the real train informed her they had just arrived at *Nationaltheatret Station*.

She walked briskly towards the exit. Outside she noticed that Tobias, her one-night stand busker and his guitar had come back to his usual spot by the fountain. A little bit taller than her, with short blond hair carefully combed aside, looked as handsome as usually. She smiled in his direction as she walked. Although it looked like it was about to rain, it was late summer in Norway so even for such an early morning, there was quite few tourists admiring his voice. Either that, or they just wanted to have a closer look at his cute dog Kygo. Erica had become friends with them a few years ago, as the dog kept coming to greet her. Tobias lived for his music and so they'd had the one-night stand after a gig he'd taken her to a while ago, but the boy was clearly not interested in anything more than friendship.

His song had finished, and she watched him picking up the money people had left in his guitar case. He looked up–

'Hey, Erica!' His voice rang out through the microphone and she saw him waving at her.

'Hey Tobias,' she said coming closer. 'How are you? Long-time no see.' She kneeled down to pet the dog. 'Hello my sweetie.' The black & white English Setter swung his tail affectionately.

'I'm good, I'm good. You?' The boy put down his guitar on his knee.

'Yeah, I'm alright. Still working at the museum, still living with my gran and of course, still single.'

Tobias smiled. He looked too wise for such a young man.

'You need to be patient, Ricky. Something will change soon. Adventure is just around the corner!' He laughed. She remembered how much she liked his laugh.

'Thanks, Tobias, but you know that this is not true.'

'Go check your runes, you'll see.' He smiled and winked at her. 'I'll see you around, girl.' He finished the conversation and got back to busking.

Erica was an overthinker. She couldn't help herself thinking about what Tobias had said and why it hadn't worked out between the two of them. There was just something in her life that pushed men away, but she didn't know what or why. She needed to overthink on it some more.

Instead of going straight to the ferry stop by the City Hall, she decided to grab a drink and a quick breakfast in the centre. She knew this little café, hidden in one of the alleys, just off the Olav Vs Gate, not far from where she was. The place called ‘Bohème Kafe’ was a charming coffee shop with very comfortable old-fashioned armchairs, where people could eat freshly baked pastry and hide away with their favourite book.

‘Morning, Erica. How are you, my darling?’ A cheerful, slightly chubby lady from behind the counter welcomed her. Her friendly face was covered in freckles with big pink blush on each cheek. Her hair pinned up in a braid, which looked like a crown or a halo.

‘Hi Sofie, good to see you. Can I have my usual, please?’ The girl didn’t even look at the board with the menu.

‘One salmon bagel and the biggest coffee coming right up,’ laughed the woman. ‘Take a seat, sweetheart. I’ll bring it over.’

‘Tusen takk, Sofie.’ Erica thanked her and walked over to her favourite table in the corner of the coffee shop, right by the giant window. She liked it as from there, she could watch people passing by. Some of them were always in a rush, some completely opposite.

It was already a few minutes past seven o'clock in the morning, but the coffee shop was nearly full. Most of those people Erica knew very well because she’d been coming to ‘Bohème Kafe’ since she was a little girl. Thanks to the warm, cosy and welcome atmosphere, Sofie had a lot of regulars.

‘God Morgen, Erica, how are you doing, child?’ greeted her elderly man sitting by the nearby table.

‘Very well, Mr Olsen. How are things?’ she asked with smile seeing familiar face.

‘Not too bad. Not too bad at all,’ the old man answered in a cheerful voice.

‘Please, give my best to Mrs Olsen,’ said the girl and nodded, politely finishing conversation.

Erica looked around. One wall was covered in bookshelves from floor to ceiling containing what seemed like all the titles in the world. However, she has decided to choose a chair to her right, so she could face an opposite wall, which was full of photographs of the café owners and their friends and family, as well as pictures painted by local artists. Among them there was one particular, which always caught Erica’s attention. Two smiling young girls looked out at her from the picture. She shook her head and grabbed a book from her bag.

In that moment Sofie showed up with her coffee and breakfast and placed it in front of the girl. She looked at the cover of the book in Erica’s hand.

‘*The Magical Language of Runes*,’ Sofie read the title out loud. ‘Your mum would be proud of you. You’re just like her.’ She looked at the same photograph of the smiling girls and added: ‘I miss her too.’

Erica smiled and said, ‘I always assumed she was interested in Vikings and their life. But never really knew how much.’

‘Look at your ring, Erica.’ Sofie took a seat opposite her.

‘I know it belonged to Mum,’ she said, turning the ring on her finger. ‘But Gran said she got it from Dad when he proposed.’

‘Yes. But you’re forgetting that both of your parents were historians. Even though Vikings were your mum’s field, your dad knows about them as well. And don't forget, this is our heritage. The whole nation’s.’

‘You meant he *knew* not knows,’ Erica corrected Sofie.

‘Ah. Honey, you do know that he is still alive, right? He left you after your mum’s death, but he is somewhere. And he’s still your father.’

‘For me he might as well be dead,’ she said, darkly.

Sofie sighed, stood up, kissed the top of Erica’s head and disappeared behind the counter.

The breakfast in front of Erica was getting cold but talking to her dead mum's best friend always made her nostalgic. She grabbed the giant mug of coffee, took a sip and drifted away. She started to think how much she liked her job at the Viking Ship Museum, where she was a curator. She wished her mum could see how she'd turned out. She had been passionate about history, particularly Vikings and their lives, ever since she was a little girl, but she never expected to get this far in her career. She was barely in her thirties. She took another sip of her coffee and looked at the clock on the wall. 'Oh helvete,' she said. 'I'm late!' She quickly left the café.

Chapter 3

On warm summer days like this day, Erica would usually take a ferry to the Bygdøy Island instead of the bus, even though sometimes the journey was longer. Before she'd set out, that morning, it looked as if it was going to rain, but Mother Nature had changed her mind and the sun appeared shyly from behind the clouds.

She sat on the ferry boat and looked right ahead. All the fjords looked really calm. This was her time to switch off her mind and dream. Dream about anything, both real and unreal. These were the kinds of thoughts that came to her: her career – maybe one day publishing her own book; her love life – maybe one crazy day to find someone who not only would she like, but who would like her back. The book would be on Vikings but the 'special someone' was for the future to decide.

Erica was not always one of the first employees to get to the Vikingship Museum where she worked, but she made sure to arrive before any visitors. She was the museum's curator, so it wasn't really her duty to do the guided tours – they had people to do that – but she always liked a little stroll just before any patrons came in, to admire the ships and artefacts.

The Vikingship Museum in Oslo was definitely not the biggest museum in the world, it was probably one of the smallest, but the charm and atmosphere inside made people want to learn. They liked to picture the Vikings taking the longships on journeys and conquering foreign lands.

She liked her job as curator. She had the privilege to work with some of the most accomplished archaeologists in the world. And she was especially pleased to have designed this exhibition. It was unique, as no other museum was in a possession of that many well preserved artefacts from the Viking Age. It was ironic but, unlike the

Vikings she loved so much, Erica had never been abroad. It's not that she didn't want to or that she wasn't curious – oh, she was curious – it's just somehow it never happened. Maybe because she'd turned her passion for history into work and managed to get where she was all before she turned thirty. There wasn't anything better in the world than being paid for something you love, that you're passionate about.

Erica was just finishing her morning stroll when she noticed him. The mysterious Wednesday Guy. Sitting in the museum's left wing on his usual little fold-out stool, with a drawing pad in hands and eyes focused on The Oseberg Ship. He looked as if nothing else existed in the world. She stopped in her tracks and watched him. His long blond shiny hair, his ideal, ideal, ideal body – even sat down she could tell that he was tall. She saw him lean forward, as if to find a new detail in the ship, then lean back and start sketching again. He smiled to himself. He had this amazing smile that made the girl think: *he is perfect.*

She wanted to go over, say hi, introduce herself. She wanted to get to know him. She wanted to see if he was even worth all this thinking and dreaming on her part. But she didn't. As much as Erica was a quite popular person in her city's social life, and as much as anyone watching her from distance thought her very confident, the truth was she was… well, quite the opposite. For all her bravado, she was genuinely shy around guys. The thought of approaching him and starting a conversation, any conversation, terrified her. She ran scenarios through her head:

'Hi, I'm Erica,' she said, hand outstretched. 'We usually just say "hi", but I thought I'd come on over today.' She smiled brightly. The young man looked at her, confused.

'Sorry?' he said.

'I'm Erica. I work here. You've seen me before…'

The man glanced around, unsure why she'd singled him out.

'Okay,' he said, then as if it were an answer to a question added: 'Hi?' Then he shrugged and went back to his drawing.

'I – I thought you might like to go and have a coffee sometime… er?'

The Wednesday Guy turned his beautiful blue eyes toward her and said: 'Coffee?'

'Yes,' Erica smiled.

'I don't drink coffee,' he answered, flatly. He turned back to his work, his shoulders tensing beneath his tight shirt.

'Oh? Oh, okay, maybe lunch then, or drinks?'

He sighed and turned back. 'Look,' he said, 'I'm sure, perhaps, you're a nice girl,' his top lip sort of curled as he said it, 'But to be honest, I'm not into this – it's all a bit forward, don't you think? I like to ask a girl out myself, and really, you're not my type. So, if it's okay by you, I'll get back to my work now. I've got a deadline.'

But of course, this didn't happen. It was all in Erica's head. She shuddered and shook the scenario out of her mind. Better to be safe, than sorry. She passed him by just at the point he was looking around and caught his eye. He smiled a warm smile and said 'hi'. Maybe she was wrong. She wasn't even sure who smiled first, but he smiled. His blue eyes, sparkling and happy.

She carried on back to her office and recreated the whole scene over a cup of coffee – she walking, he turning, them saying 'hi', he smiling, she smiling. She ran it a hundred times over in her head and was ready to do it again when a knock on the door interrupted her.

'Hey Rick, are you busy?' A tall girl with long ginger hair poked her head around the door.

'Hey Matilde, no, not at all. Come on in.' She encouraged the girl with a hand gesture to take a seat. 'What's going on?'

Matilde worked in acquisitions. She was a bit younger than Erica and pretty too. Erica liked her. They'd been friends for a long time.

‘Just wanted to ask about tonight,’ Matilde said. ‘Are you working late, again, and will you be going to the concert straight from here or do you have time for few drinks before?’ They were going to see ‘Sapphire Moonlight’ at ‘Svart’ in the evening. Matilde was looking forward to it.

She looked around the room. She’d been to Erica’s office many times, but never actually had time to notice things – she was always in and out, grabbing a signature, asking a quick question, she didn’t have time for details. For example, she knew that one entire wall was covered in books, but she just never noticed that they were pretty much every single book ever written about Vikings and their lives. And not only academic books, but magazines, too: *History*, *National Geographic*, even *Marvel* comics with Thor bursting out of the cover.

She picked up a battered comic and turned to Erica:

‘Did you ever picture Thor would look like Chris Hemsworth?’ she said. ‘God, he’s hot!’ She saw Erica blush and chuckled. Then she added: ‘Speaking of hot, have you noticed that guy coming here and drawing ships?’

‘What guy?’ Erica lied, her face getting redder.

‘You know what guy. He would be perfect for you, Rick!’

‘Yeah, anyway drinks… err yeah drinks before are good for me,’ she blustered. ‘Actually, I’m a bit busy now, let’s chat later? In the pub?’ Erica shuffled some papers on her desk as if she were really busy. She wasn’t going to gossip about guys – hot or not – especially when she was sober. The situation would look completely different in just a few hours and a few beers later.

The two young women met in the pub in Grünerløkka district. Regular customers, they knew everyone who worked there by name. By day, ‘Svart’ was serving lunch and it was a quiet and perfect place to sit in the beer garden and enjoy a drink by the river. By night, it throbbed with live music. Most of the customers were locals of all ages. Very occasionally a few tourists accidentally discovered it. Tonight, it was full of familiar faces.

They'd been there 30 minutes and two beers already and Erica was feeling chilled. She stood up and suddenly said: 'You're right, Matilde, that guy is hot.' She took off across the room.

'Hey! You can't just tell me that and walk away! Who? Who's hot?' her friend yelled after her.

Erica laughed and waved a hand, dismissively. A few minutes later, she came back with a small tray full of tequila shots. 'The guy from the museum,' she said.

Her friend looked blanked and lifted a glass and a lime wedge. 'What guy?'

'The Wednesday Guy?' said Erica, shaking her head. 'Draws the Oseberg Ship?'

'Aahhh, him,' Matilda beamed. 'He's perfect.'

Erica laughed, nodded and said:

'Oh helvete, I've been dying to talk to someone about him forever.'

'Really?'

'Yeah, and since you started it this afternoon, you can listen to me going on about him all night!' She grinned and raised a shot glass. 'Skål! To imaginary love!'

Someone from a neighbouring table overheard her and repeated: 'Cheers! To imaginary love!'

The main band would be on soon and the place was getting fuller. When Matilde came back with another round of beers, something happened. Something amazing. Something that Erica thought only happened in books or the movies. Or her dreams.

Squeezing through the crowd, a man with a very familiar smile caught her eye. She actually grabbed the table for support.

Oh, helvete, she thought. 'He's coming over!'

He reached her table. As usual, he smiled. She smiled and said hi. Then something else happened. This perfect man not only said 'hi' back but added: 'How are you?' as if it was just normal and not the most amazing thing.

How am I? Erica thought, astonished. *How am I? This is amazing!* But everything was happening so fast and Erica was already a good few drinks in, she responded ridiculously politely and replied: 'I'm very well, thank you. How are you doing?'

She waited for his response. In her merry state, she saw him look blank, heard him murmur something and watched him walk away.

Shit! Suddenly, she was angry at herself. Tipsy and angry. *What the hell? How? Why? What?* She'd been waiting months for this moment and now – what? She wasn't really sure what just happened. Maybe he hadn't been talking to her? Maybe she'd misheard what he said. *Was that even really him?* She shook her head, trying to clear it up.

'Hey, I'm Bjørn,' came a familiar voice. The Wednesday Guy had come back! 'This is Carl, may we sit here?' he asked, pointing at the end of the bench.

Erica was speechless. Matilde – wing woman extraordinaire – took over, introduced themselves and encouraged the boys to take a seat.

'You look familiar,' she said, smiling brightly. 'Aren't you the guy who comes to the museum? You draw ships, right?'

Bjørn smiled his amazing smile. 'Yeah, yeah I do.' He looked over Erica.

She looked as if she'd been hit by lightning and was melting away.

Matilde grabbed Erica's hand. 'Excuse us,' she said and dragged her to the restrooms. Once inside she thumped her friend across the chest. Hard.

'Hey!' yelled Erica.

'What on earth, Rick? That's him! That's the hot guy who looks like human Thor!'

Erica wobbled and said nothing.

'This is your chance, girl!' said Matilde.

‘I don’t know…’

Matilde squealed. ‘Don’t know what! What’s not to know? He’s clearly into you! Practically stalking! Get out there and stop acting like a schoolgirl!’

Erica hesitated, she was just about to sneak out, but she finally gave up and said that she’d try.

‘Try?’ said Matilde. ‘Okay, you go and ‘try’, but ‘try’ properly or I’ll kill you.’ She started to push her laughing friend out the door. Then she pulled her back, quickly.

‘What’s wrong?’ said Erica, puzzled.

‘I need the toilet,’ laughed Matilde. ‘Won’t be long.’

Back at the table, one of the boys had bought a round of shots for them all.

‘To unexpected meetings, skål!’ Bjørn raised his shot glass and winked to Erica.

Erica smiled at him. After that any awkwardness and shyness on her part was history. It turned out, not only was he incredibly attractive but funny and smart too. In fact, he was so easy to talk to, that they missed the gig completely.

When Erica and Bjørn were getting into the cab, her ears buzzing with all the chatter and her heart pounding with what was to come, she knew one thing for sure: Wednesdays would never be the same.

Chapter 4

Roger was home and done for the night. Today had been a long and busy day – too many meetings, too much talking, too much smiling at people who couldn't pour out a bucket of water if the instructions were on the bottom. It was only natural he went to a nearby bar to unwind, and only natural he should get talking to the loveliest woman there, and only natural he just said goodbye to her, waving her off at the door with a kiss and a soft smile.

He yawned, put the dirty wine glasses into dishwasher and turned off the light in the kitchen. He was just about to go to get ready for bed proper, when the front doorbell rang.

Weird, he thought turning around halfway up the stairs, *Maybe she forgot something.*

The doorbell rang again. Quietly but insistently.

'I'm coming, I'm coming,' he murmured. 'God, people can be so impatient.'

He switched on the small lamp beside the mirror in the hallway and opened the stained-glass door with a charming smile. It melted in the face of a rather short, chubby man in his eighties, not the beautiful leggy blonde he'd seen off at the door a few moments earlier. The man was completely soaked.

'Yes?' Roger asked through the slightly opened door. 'Can I help you?' His free hand tried blindly to find the cricket bat he kept in the umbrella stand just in case.

'Apologies for such a late visit, sir. I am looking for Mr Roger Wright.'

Roger looked at him with suspicion. Who was he? Had something happened at the museum?

'That's me, what is it about? Did something happen?'

'Ah, sort of.' The man took his wet bowler hat off his head and added: 'You see, my name is David Evans.'

Roger looked blank. Then he remembered something

from family meetings. 'Evans? As in *Evans & Sons*?'

'Ah, that is correct, sir. I am one of your family lawyers. May I come in? It's rather wet out.'

Roger became a little more suspicious, so he was glad deep inside that he'd managed to find the bat and held it tight in his hand. 'Forgive me, but I have met my family lawyers quite few times in my life–'

'Ah, such as when you inherited this house?' The old man smiled in a pleasant way and passed his business card:

Evans & Sons Ltd §

David Evans

Attorney of Law

W1J 8AJ London

In the corner of the card was a special symbol which Roger recognised instantly. He put the bat back to the umbrella stand and opened the door. He didn't really know what the symbol meant and indeed if it had *any* meaning at all, but he knew that the old law companies had a specially agreed symbol with each of their clients. Only members of either the Evans' or the Wright's family would know it. Roger's family were very old customers indeed.

'Please, you'd better come in,' he invited the visitor inside. 'Would you like a cup of tea?'

Mr Evans took off his coat, sat down in the living room and put rather vintage briefcase he was carrying right next to him on the sofa. He felt damp. His host was around the corner in the kitchen preparing beverages. He looked around and thought that it was a cute little place; a mixture of old style and modern. The kitchen/dining room and living room were all connected – open space. Not too big but definitely spacious for one, two people. Mr Evans hazarded a guess that the bedroom, bathroom and perhaps one more room were on the first floor above them. There were stairs in the corner. Family pictures on the fireplace were but none of them was a wedding picture. Maybe Mr Evans was old-fashioned, but he observed in every single house he had ever visited, that if someone was married, there was at least one picture to remember that day. So, Mr Wright had not yet found Ms Right? Mr Evans allowed a little chuckle.

'Tea.' He placed two mugs of tea on the coasters on the coffee table. 'I'm sorry, did you want sugar?'

'Ah no, no sugar, thank you.' Mr Evans smiled.

Roger sat on the armchair opposite him. He looked at the solicitor, trying really, really hard to remind himself of the old man's face. It did look a little bit familiar, but on the other hand he just knew that he had never ever met the man before. The lawyer was wearing what looked like a very expensive suit. He wasn't nervous, quite opposite in fact, calm with a slight excitement in his eyes. An old wooden clock in the living room just announced that it was 10 p.m. and in some kind of weird and creepy coincidence, outside it thundered.

'So, Mr Wright–' the man began.

'Professor,' corrected Roger.

'I do beg your pardon, Professor Wright. You must wonder, what an old stranger is doing in your house at this time of night.'

'I will not deny it, Mr Evans, I do. You do you look very familiar, yet I've never met you before, have I?'

Mr Evans smiled again. 'Ah, I'm afraid you're quite right, Professor Wright. I know you as young Roger. May I call you Roger?' the professor nodded approval; the old man continued. 'You have met my son and my grandson.'

Maybe the family resemblance was what was so familiar.

'They were the lawyers reading the testament of my grandfather who left me this house?' he said.

'Ah, yes. I, myself retired years ago but…' He paused and took a sip of tea. 'I have one more special delivery before I die. You see, I am in possession of certain deliverables that my father told me of and that was passed on to me. I wanted to deliver it myself in person.'

Roger looked at him with curiosity. He had absolutely no clue what this was about. The family lawyer coming here, to his house, this late and talking about special deliveries. He wondered, if perhaps his grandfather left him something else, but what was all the mystery about?

'Without making this more complicated than it should be, Professor. Your great-grandfather, Sir Roger Wright – God rest his soul – before his sudden death at quite a young age, left this letter to my father. He was Sir Roger's lawyer back in the time. He said our firm was to deliver it on this very day to his final heir–' the thunder clamoured on cue outside.

'Final heir?' said Roger.

'Ah, you, Professor, you.' The solicitor took a sip of his drink and added, 'Indeed. I must say, this is delicious tea.'

'It's builder's tea,' said Roger staring at the briefcase.

Mr David Evans finished his tea, took out the envelope from his briefcase, put it on the table, shook Roger's hand and with just a brief saying 'good luck' saw himself out.

Less than an hour ago, Roger was tired and ready for bed. Right now, he stood all by himself in his living room, widely awake, staring at the white envelope lying on his coffee table. He slowly took it in his hands, sat back on the armchair, took a deep breath and decided to open it.

The letter was addressed in handwriting and the black ink said: '*To Roger Wright, my descendant.*'

Roger carefully peeled off the red wax. The paper inside was green, clearly custom made. He started to read:

London, September 1908

My Dearest Roger,

I hope this letter will find you well. I am fully aware that this might sound a little bit odd, the letter coming from your great-grandfather like it was from beyond this world, but this is real. I assure you in this. You see, when I am writing this very own letter, it is 111 years from where you are right now. Times have changed, people were born and died. I probably cannot even imagine in what times you are living. Let me tell you a story, which I hope will clarify the purpose of this letter and my hopes. I believe you know that I was an archaeologist. Not bragging, but quite successful. One day, after years of searching the legendary Einarr's tomb, I finally came across it. I already knew that my time on this world (even though I am still young and just expecting my very first child) is limited. You see, medicine now is not as advanced as it probably is in your times, or as least I shall hope so. After all those years of excavations and researches, I knew almost instantly after opening the grave, that it was not a tomb I have been looking for. You must remember though, the times I am living in, are not so cheerful anymore. Queen Victoria died just few years ago. People struggle with money, health and living. So, the treasure and discovery were something, that people could think of and put their minds aside of the regular life. The excitement. As I mentioned before, seeing the whole treasure up close, I have realized at once it was not the one, but this is what people wanted and needed. I never said a word, not even to my close friend Mayor Anderson. I struggled for days asking myself 'what to do'. Should I tell anyone the truth? Or perhaps not say anything? And then I have *reminded myself an old friend I met during my studies. She was at the time making her career as a fortune teller. So, the next day I have decided to visit her, in her own little shop in Covent Garden. She was using a variety of objects and possessed incredible knowledge but was an expert in runes reading especially. I asked her 'What shall I do, I have no time to finish my task' and the runes told me to leave it. To enjoy last few days with my beloved wife and that my descendant of the same name and the same passion to history, in exactly 111 years will know what to do.*

'That's nonsense,' gasped Roger and put the letter down. He stood up and started to walk around the room, talking out loud like he was giving a lecture to someone that it's an absurd and it is really not funny to involve dead members of his family in a prank. After short moment he thought *'What if this isn't a joke. Mr Evans looked quite serious,'* picked up the letter and continued to read.

You must also wonder, how did I realize, that this was not Einarr. Many people know the old Vikings saga about the brothers and the rings. But not many knows what happened after their arrival in England. When I heard of it for the very first time, I was just a boy. The thought of adventure was so fascinating, I decided to join a group of elderly amateurs, or I shall say the treasure hunters. One summer few PhD students from university somewhere in Norway, came to London to try their luck.

On the last evening after few drinks, they told us everything they knew about saga and the treasure. That was the first time someone ever mentioned a map. A map made by the Vikings who buried Einarr and their treasure with him, so after things would calm down between them and Anglo-Saxons, one of them could come back, find it and take it home. So, when in the tomb I discovered, there was indeed some kind of encrypted map I knew, that this warrior was only searching for the treasure left by his people. I took the map, donated rest of the valuables we found to the British Museum and here we are.

My Dearest Roger,

I turned to Runes in search for advice and help. I am following their wisdom and enclose the map with this letter. Remember, the symbols on it are not Anglo-Saxon runes, so you might need some help. One more thing. Find Vegvisir. He is the key.

Respectfully Yours,

Sir Roger Wright

Roger put the letter down on his knees, made a very serious face and said out loud to himself, *'Wait a minute. If that wasn't Einarr's tomb, where is it then? Also, who on earth is Vegvisir?'*

Chapter 5

It was still very early in the morning when Erica has realized someone was shaking her body and tried to wake her up. The voice kept repeating her name and there was this other weird sound too, like a fly buzzing. She finally opened her eyes, only to discover that a naked Bjørn was lying next to her, holding a pillow over his head to cover his ears with one hand, and with the other, was gently nudging her back.

'Huh?' she mumbled, then suddenly realised the weird noise was her own phone.

'Nnnn…' said Bjørn under the pillow. She reached for her phone, grabbed a random T-shirt from the floor and got up.

'Hello?' she whispered, leaving the bedroom.

'Hello there,' said a very English voice on the other end. It was a deep voice, pleasant to hear even this early. 'Apologies for calling so early, but it's rather urgent. I'm looking for a Doctor Erica Skyberg? Hello? Can you hear me?'

'Yeah, hi, sorry,' Erica said rubbing her sleepy eyes. She started to walk towards the kitchen trying not to disturb the sleeping Bjørn in the other room. 'I'm Doctor Skyberg. Can I help you?' She listened to the voice for a few seconds then added, 'Excuse me? What!'

The phone call lasted only three minutes, but Erica felt that her brain would explode any second. She didn't really know if it was because of the conversation she'd just had or because she was still a little bit drunk heading into a hangover, but the world was suddenly very strange. She looked around for a TV.

'Is everything okay?' Bjørn said from the doorway. 'You weren't coming back for a good amount of time, so I just wanted to check if everything was fine.' He smiled and sat on the chair on the opposite side of the kitchen table.

'Yes, thanks.' Erica looked startled, and before he had a chance to say anything else, asked. 'Where is your TV, you do have a TV, right?'

Bjørn pointed behind her. In a small but cosy living room was sofa and the very large TV. She jumped up from the chair and still without any explanation turned on the set. She didn't even need to flick through the channels. She pressed a very well-known channel for her, number '42'. International news. Then she noticed the T-shirt as it wasn't quite as big as she thought it would be, pulled it to cover her up as much as it could and sat down on the sofa with a plonk. *'This is what he was talking about,'* she thought, her eyes wide open. She turned the volume up. Bjørn sat down next to her.

The BBC was showing the most important parts from an already very short press conference, which had been held the night before in the British Museum in London. A few gentlemen stood on the marble steps in front of small crowd of reporters. A youngish, tallish, ginger-haired guy was currently speaking. The screen labelled him Detective Charles O'Sullivan of Scotland Yard. Erica watched this very serious man, who wasn't even bothered by the flashes coming from cameras right in his face as he spoke. At the bottom of the screen the rolling headline white on the red background said:

Breaking News: Shooting and theft at British Museum.
One person dead.

'The investigation is in progress, anyone in possession of any information, both on the missing Einarr's ring and on this brutal murder, please contact the police. We have established a hotline for any witnesses coming forward. We will not rest until we find the persons responsible for this terrible act. Our thoughts are with Mike's family and we are sorry for their loss.' He stepped back and another man came forward.

Roger cleared his throat and said 'This is a great loss. Mike was the security guard here for many years. He will be greatly missed,' said the professor and added this time, a description of the missing object. A few pictures of the ring flashed up on the screen.

'Isn't that your ring?' Bjørn, who was now snuggled on the sofa with Erica, pointed to the screen.

'Yeah, it looks like the one I have,' she glanced at her hand. 'Although mine, of course, is a reproduction.'

The press conference finished and the BBC moved on to another story. Erica turned off TV. Then it hit her:

'I've never been abroad. Like never! For Odin's sake, I've never even left Oslo!' she was suddenly panicked. 'What if I'll get lost at the airport? What if I don't find the right plane? What if–' she stood up and started to pace back and forth.

'Erica, calm down. What on earth are you talking about? Why are you so panicked?' said Bjørn. 'Here, I'll make coffee and breakfast. What happened in that phone call?' he grabbed her by her shoulders, sat her back on the sofa, kissed on the top of her head and went away to the kitchen. She watched him in a sort of daze. She was silent for a while not because of trying to get her head around the unexpected events of that morning, but because she suddenly realised where she was.

She was in the Wednesday Guy's apartment.

She had spent night in here with the beautiful Wednesday Guy himself. The Wednesday Guy who was now wearing just a pair of grey sweats and was making breakfast. For her. Erica pinched herself and took a deep breath in. Bacon and mushrooms. She loved bacon and mushrooms.

'Eggs?' asked Bjørn. She loved eggs, too. She nodded eagerly. Bjørn smiled and said: 'Phone call?'

'Oh. Yes,' said Erica. She took in another breath, let it out and started to talk.

‘The guy on the phone was the curator of medieval section from British Museum. Sorry if I woke you up by the way. Anyway, I didn’t really catch his name, but he was going on about this missing ring. He said it was urgent, and he wants me to go over there.’

Bjørn looked up from the eggs. ‘There?’

‘I’m supposed to be in London tomorrow,’ Erica said.

Bjørn brought her over a mug of coffee. ‘That’s it? No more details?’ he asked.

‘Nope.’ She took a sip, it tasted good. ‘No more details.’

Chapter 6

'Gran? Granny!' Erica came home later than usual. Even though she wanted to share the news with her grandmother and ask her opinion about whether or not she should go to London, she needed to take care of few things at work. 'Gran? Where are you?'

'I'm on the patio,' the voice coming through the open garden door informed the girl.

Erica went to the kitchen, grabbed two beers from the fridge and made her way outside.

'Oh, there you are,' she said to her gran passing her an open bottle. 'I have some news to share.'

Her grandmother was sitting on a swing bench under a blanket with a sudoku in her hand. She took off her reading glasses, took the bottle and made some space for Erica to sit down. It was a warm, summer evening. The light on the patio wasn't too bright, and all the stars were already visible. The whole neighbourhood was so quiet, that only a few insects flying around could be heard.

'Did something bad happen, honey?' asked Greta. She combed her granddaughter's hair with her fingers. Erica looked at her and sort of smiled, not sure what to make of the day.

'No. Yes. No. Both? I mean, there was a theft at the British Museum! In London.'

'Wait, what?' said Greta.

Erica nodded and carried on with the story: 'There was a robbery last night and one of the security guards died at the scene!'

Greta was shocked. 'So, what was so precious that was worth a man's life?'

'A ring,' said Erica. 'Found in a Viking tomb a hundred years ago. It is missing from the museums display.'

Greta stopped stroking her hair. 'You mean the cursed one from the saga of Einarr?' She took a sip of her beer and paused. 'Was it worth anything? Apart from that it was a symbol from this story?'

Erica shrugged. 'It had two very valuable gemstones. Probably that was the reason.'

'Still…' said Greta. 'What does it have to do with you?'

Erica told her granny about the phone call from the curator. She told her about the doubts regarding her trip. She went to the kitchen once more to grab another two bottles of beer. It was already 9 p.m. and she still hadn't made up her mind. She'd even flipped her lucky coin to check where her heart was at.

'That's it!' Greta put her near empty bottle on the ground, stood up and went inside. 'This is huge, my darling!' she called behind her as she walked. 'And *huge* deserves a proper celebration!' She swung open the fridge door, grabbed a bottle of champagne and two glasses and went to the girl's room.

'Let's pack your suitcase because you, honey, are going to London!'

***

And now she was waiting for a lift to the airport.

It's funny how sometimes life can turn 360 degrees without even a little warning. For weeks Erica had had a crush in this one guy and here he was waiting for her in his car right outside her home in Holmenkollen. As soon as she had decided to go to England, Bjørn insisted on seeing her one more time. His idea, not hers. The plan was to go to a restaurant on the way to the airport and spend some time together in daylight, sober. They'd get to know each other and see if there is any potential there. Long term.

Erica couldn't believe it. Not only was the guy good looking but so far he was ticking all the boxes. All of them. Funny, smart, he loved history, art, nature and the outdoors, sport, music, cultural events, kind, and to finish the list, he even volunteered in the animal shelter. Too good to be true. At the restaurant Erica drank her coffee and looked at him, wondering what was wrong with him. *Perfect does not exist,* she thought. *This is just impossible.*

'Coffee's good,' she said. *Maybe you've got some annoying habits? Or you're a player? Or some dark secret?* Her brain screamed.

Bjørn nodded and smiled his lovely smile.

Or, she thought, *for now I can just drop it and take him as he is. Perfect.*

***

'Final call for flight D82803 to London Gatwick. Please make your way to gate 27 as quickly as possible.' The announcer's voice came through the speakers at the departure's hall of Oslo Gardermoen airport. Erica had said goodbye to Bjørn. She'd wanted to spend as much time with him as she could, so now she was officially late for her flight.

She ran through the airport as fast as she could. She was not really the athletic type, even though her long legs and skinny posture could easily mislead you.

'This is a passenger announcement: Could Miss Erica Skyberg, I repeat, Miss Erica Skyberg, please go to gate no. 27. This is the final call,' said the same tinny, high-pitched voice.

'God, that's me!' yelled Erica. 'Move it, people, move it!' She was shouting like a crazy woman, trying not to run into people. 'I'm here! I'm here!'

A very smiley stewardess, clearly feeling sorry for Erica and her dishevelled appearance, reached out for her boarding card.

'We were just about to close the door, Miss Skyberg! Welcome aboard.'

'OMG, I made it!' laughed Erica, her carry on getting in the way.

She settled into her seat. The take-off was easy but as soon as the captain switched the seatbelt sign off, she went to the bathroom. The truth was that she was not only looking terrible but feeling it as well. The hangover from drinking with Gran finally kicked in. All her breakfast, and the good coffee, ended up in the toilet. She looked in the mirror and started to feel sorry for herself as well. What she saw, was a thirty-two-year old woman with huge black circles under her eyes, messy short platinum hair and vomit in the corner of her mouth.

'And I am a curator at a prestigious museum?' Sometimes she couldn't believe it. She cleaned herself up a little, scrunched her hair, wiped her eyes and left the bathroom to go back to her seat.

Although the plane was full and everyone on the board seemed to be minding their own business, a man on a row over was clearly staring at her. And that was it. She knew right then that even though she had only just met Bjørn, she was already falling in love with him. She knew because if someone threw even a little attention at her, say a passenger on a plane, she'd already have pictured their wedding. But not this time. All she could think about was perfect Bjørn. Erica apologised to the people in her row as she stepped over them and without giving the stranger any attention, sat back in her seat by the window. She was too hungover to read anything, so she closed her eyes in the hope she would get some sleep. Behind her two elderly ladies were chatting loudly.

'Did you hear what happened in the British Museum?' one said.

'Yes, poor guy. Shocking. I hope they catch whoever did this.'

'Awful. What were they after?' said her friend.

'This is what it says in the paper, look…' One of the ladies grabbed a newspaper from her bag and passed it over. The woman started to read it quietly.

Erica's eyes snapped open and she started to panic. She didn't even know much about the case! Yes, she was a curator and yes, she specialized in Vikings, but there was so little known about Einarr and his curse that she really had no idea why on earth they called her. It hit her again: she was jetting off to a foreign country, somewhere she'd never been to before. And of course, it happened when she'd just met someone. And okay, she was going to help solve the robbery, but she wasn't a detective so really why was she going?

She stood up from her seat and turning back to the lady behind her said, 'Excuse me? Could I see your paper for a second?'

The woman had just finished reading. 'Well, yes,' she said.

The massive red text on the front page, **Breaking News: Theft and Murder at the British Museum**, was surely getting every reader's attention. Inside the report showed a few pictures of the museum, the stolen object and the security guard with his family. He was called Mike. Erica took a closer look at his smiley face. He was holding his son on his arms, and his wife and daughter were standing next to him. He was in his uniform. She read the article about five times and eventually gave the newspaper back.

'Coffee? Tea? Refreshments?' The stewards shuffled along offering food and drink. Erica ordered a coffee. A minute later she leaned over and asked the lady behind her for the newspaper yet again.

The woman kindly gave it to her and said, 'Here, love. You can keep it.'

Chapter 7

Professor Roger Wright stood outside the closed conference door, in the middle of the empty hallway, in one of the many wings at the enormous building of the British Museum. He was wondering what is going to happen next. He didn't even know the exact reason for this meeting. He could only assume that it was regarding the recent not so pleasant events. The theft, murder and the missing ring. He had no clue whatsoever, if the Board was angry with him, blaming him for what it has happened, or just want to chat and see if he could be any help to Scotland Yard with the ongoing investigation.

He was about to knock on the door, but his fist for some reason, stopped just a few centimetres away from its surface. *Why am I so nervous? I didn't do anything for God's sake!* He scolded himself in his thoughts and looked around. It was the middle of a day but there was not even one person passing by. He lowered his hand and decided to grab a cup of water from the nearby dispenser. His throat was dry.

Suddenly the conference door opened.

'Oh, you are already here, Professor. Excellent!' One of the Board members invited him in with a great gesture. 'Please come inside.'

All the other members of the museum's Board were already settled in around the big oval conference table, waiting his arrival.

'S-sorry, am I late?' Roger, confused, looked at his watch and then back at the people gathered in the room. He scanned the faces. Something wasn't quite right. *Why is this Scotland Yard detective in here? What does he want from me? Why do I suddenly feel guilty?*

'No, no, no, come on in, Professor. You're not late. Our morning meeting ran over.' One quickly responded and pointed at empty chair. 'Please.'

It was another sunny day in London, the blinds were shut, so when the lights went off, the only visibility in the room was thanks to the bright Power Point presentation on the projector's screen. The current slide was showing the stolen ring with the caption: *Einarr's ring found in London, UK by Sir R. Wright. 1908.*

Roger sitting in an uncomfortable conference room chair looked at the screen and smiled to himself. As a member of the Wright family he had been familiar with this discovery since he was a little boy. It was his great-grandfather who found this mysterious tomb belonging to the Viking hero called Einarr and the great treasure buried with him. The story of how he decided to donate everything to the museum instead of making profit out of it was something that was taught in history lessons in schools. For Roger, though, it was even more personal. He had inherited not only the first and last name of this great archaeologist but his passion for history as well.

Oh, and good looks. Yes, the great archaeologist Sir Roger Wright and the curator Professor Roger Wright were blood related indeed.

'Ehm–' The chairman cleared his throat to let everyone in the room know it was time to stop chattering and proceed with the meeting. He turned to the man at his side, the one Roger had been suspicious of. 'Charles, oh, I mean Detective O'Sullivan, would you care to begin?'

The ginger man nodded at him, 'Yes, thank you, Chairman Applegate.' He turned slightly to look at the curator. 'Professor Wright, do you know anything that we might have missed? Something that could help us to solve the case?' His slightly irritated voice under his Irish accent sounded like he was accusing Roger of something. Or at least suspecting that the professor was hiding something. He appeared to want to show him that this was not a game.

Roger stared at him.

'I'm sorry, is this some kind of not formal interrogation, Detective? In a Board Room? Am I a suspect?' He looked around at the faces. 'Could someone explain me what on earth is going on in here?' he said angrily, protecting himself.

'You are not a suspect,' said the chairman with a smooth smile. 'Please excuse Detective O'Sullivan–' he gave Charlie a telling off look then turned back to Roger. 'But do try to understand. The case is urgent. A man is dead, a good colleague. And we don't know if the thief got everything he wanted, or if he's coming back.'

'Okay, I understand that, but how am I involved?' Professor looked a little confused and wounded. He'd liked Mike. His wife always baked him cookies for his birthday.

'Wasn't it your ancestor that discovered the ring in the first place?' Charlie growled, interrupting him. 'Is this some kind of 'Wright family' scam gone bad, perhaps?'

'No, sir, it is not!' said Roger, half rising from his seat. He gave a laugh to show the nonsense he was hearing. 'I am doing everything in my power to find the ring and who is behind this crime.' Mike was the longest-serving guard at the museum. They used to joke he was becoming an exhibit.

'Are you, now? And how are you planning on doing that?' Detective O'Sullivan continued to speak in his mocking manner. 'Perhaps just slip everything back and pretend nothing's happened?'

'Wait, what?' Roger shot up with such anger and speed that the chair he was sitting on fell backwards. 'That's absurd and out of order!' He was face to face with the policeman.

The chairman stepped between them and said with a very serious look: 'Professor, the company's card – your card – was used to buy plane tickets, a hotel room and a number of other expenses.'

Roger looked shocked. Chairman Applegate continued: 'I am going to ask this only once: were you helping the thief with the robbery and to escape the country?'

Roger folded his arms and tightened his jaw. 'Sir, in a word, no.' Roger put his hands together and for a moment it looked like he was praying. 'Let me explain. Time is of the essence here and everything has happened so quickly that it slipped my mind to mention it to you yesterday. I have invited a curator from Norway to London to help us,' he looked at his watch, 'actually she will be landing any minute.'

'What?' said the chairman. 'What woman?'

'She is one of the foremost specialists in Vikings in Norway. The plane, the hotel is for her!'

'How can she help us?' growled the detective. He had a feeling there was something the professor wasn't saying.

Roger looked at him and repeated a little slowly: 'She's an expert. She can help us–'

The chairman interrupted him. 'But, Roger, according to accounts it was not only an Oslo-London flight but first a London-Oslo. The very next morning after the theft!'

'Yes, I know. That was my mistake. My first thought was to go and meet her and ask for some help, as this robbery is clearly something to do with the ring–'

'But who is she?' spluttered Chairman Applegate.

'Professor Cox had worked with her in Oslo before he retired. When he needed help to transfer some objects for a special exhibition in the Vikingship Museum, remember? She's an expert in Viking life and their language.' Roger looked like he was calming the situation.

'I see,' said Chairman Applegate.

'Cox phoned me the day after, kindly gave me her number. So, she's coming here, instead of me going there. Simple really.' He picked up the chair from the floor and sat back down.

'The best in her field?' asked the chairman.

'Yes, sir, that is correct,' Professor Wright said with assurance in his voice.

The old man reached for his walking stick and tapped it on the floor. 'Bring her to the museum tomorrow,' he said standing up. 'Then, we will see what to do about this whole card fiasco. You should have cancelled the flight, you know.' He glared at Roger and left the room.

‘Yes, sir,’ said Roger as the rest of the members stood up and followed him without even one word. Some of them just looked at him as if they’d already agreed that he should be hanged, and nothing would change their minds. He smiled as they passed him. The detective was the last to leave, glaring at the curator. Roger nodded a short, sharp nod.

Chapter 8

It was only when the plane touched the runway of London's Gatwick airport, did it occur to Erica, that within the very brief phone conversation she'd had with the curator they have never had a chance to discuss the details of what was going to happen next.

The plane had landed, and she sat there with her seatbelt still on. She watched for a minute with curiosity how the majority of people had already stood up and started to take their luggage down, even though the plane hadn't stopped yet.

'Ladies and gentlemen, could you please return to your seats and wait for the captain to turn off the seat-belt sign?' The cabin crew manager tried to control the situation. Most people ignored her, but when the sound of phones being switched back from airplane mode resounded, the stewardess got annoyed and ordered everyone to take their seats immediately. They did as they were told.

'Phone!' laughed Erica excitedly. She entered her password, turn the data on and carefully watched the screen retrieving all his functions. *Surely there must be a message from someone. Granny? Bjørn?*

But there was none. Nothing. She felt in her heart like someone was gently pricking it with a needle saying 'nobody loves you, nobody cares'. *And what about the curator with more instructions?* she thought. Nothing. She put the phone back in her bag with obvious disappointment and looked out through the window.

It was early afternoon. The end of the summer. She was fully aware that London was one of the biggest metropoles in the world, but it looked more like she had just landed in the Caribbean. The sun was alone in the sky, so bright that without sunglasses people were forced to blink and squint. She'd forgotten her own. She looked at a few flags on the wind mast. No sign of wind at all. Already she felt hot. Her initial thought was '*faen, perfekt!*' She'd always heard so much about rainy England, that she wasn't really prepared for summer in the city. But then she quickly changed her mind. *No, not* fucking *perfect. It* will *be perfect! Not weather, nor some guy I just have met will ruin this trip. Nothing. I came here for a reason and have to enjoy this adventure while it lasts. Who knows, maybe it will change my life?* She laughed at that thought, grabbed her carry-on, said goodbye to the flight attendant and left the plane. Hot summer air hit her face.

Erica collected her luggage and made it through the passport control easily. At the arrivals hall she checked her phone yet again and started to look around.

Ping!

She got really excited when the sound of new message rang out of her pocket, but it was just her network welcoming her in the United Kingdom. After a minute of a hesitation she has decided to call the curator and ask what she should do. But no luck. The phone went straight to voicemail. Before she left Oslo, while she was waiting for Bjørn to pick her up, she'd managed to do a little research on the curator and look him up on the internet. None of the people in the arrivals hall looked like him.

She started to panic, unnecessarily. *What if there is no one to pick me up? What if I was supposed to get to the city all by myself? What if he has sent me an email? And I didn't read it? Does he even have my address? What if I'm waiting in the wrong spot? What if...*

'Erica? Miss Erica Skyberg?'

Erica looked up to see an attractive, tall, black, definitely younger than the curator guy stretching out his hand to welcome her.

'Doctor Skyberg, yes, hello. And you are…?' she moved toward him and shook his hand.

'Hello Dr Skyberg. My name's Tony. Professor Wright's PA.' He grabbed her bag, looked around to double-check it was the only bag she had, and explained:

‘Unfortunately, he’s stuck in a very important meeting with the Museum’s Board. He sends his apologies.’ It went through his head that it's quite unusual for a woman to travel with such small luggage.

‘Oh, alright,’ she said. She was just so used to being stood up by guys, that she expected it all the time. Even for work. She was perfection in pretending that nothing was wrong even though it bothered her very much. She realised she was being ridiculous. Why would Tony be lying about the professor’s whereabouts? She shrugged it off.

‘This way,’ Tony interrupted her chain of thoughts and with a hand gesture pointed the direction.

The car wasn’t parked far but walking even such a short distance in an awkward silence, made Erica feel as if they were about to walk all the way to the city themselves. Once in the car, as soon as she fastened her seatbelt, she asked Tony where she would be staying. Just to start a conversation. Tony took a long pause before answering shortly, ‘In the hotel in central London.’

She felt weird. Usually she had an instant connection with people, even strangers. The conversation flows and that gives her an opportunity to not to focus on matters she would normally if she were alone. Like, for example, the fact that she was at this moment absolutely terrified. She was indeed in England. Driving on the other side of the road. With one hand she squeezed by her seat real tight, turned around her head to her companion and used the other hand to block the view on the side. Her heart was pounding.

‘I know we just have met, Tony, but please distract me. I guess I'll need some time to get use to the differences,’ she said with a smile.

‘No problem, madam,’ said Tony turning the radio on. ‘Any music preferences?’

‘Any. And please don't call me madam. It sounds weird. I'm Erica.’

‘Yes, Dr Skyberg, no problem,’ he smiled as he knew that is not what she meant.

For the entire drive they still didn't talk much. She wasn't sure if he was intimidated by her or there was something about her that he didn't like, but at least he did listen to her wish to distract her. He managed to find his favourite radio station and sang all the way, even if he didn't quite know the lyrics.

From time to time she’d suddenly cover her eyes but as soon as the landscape outside the window has changed from green fields into city buildings, she relaxed and let the excitement take over.

‘Is this...? Are we…?’ she started to say but became speechless really quickly. Her head was turning left and right and left and right again. She wished to stop the time for a second just to have a closer look at everything they were passing by. Erica couldn’t sit still. If anyone was watching her from a distance, they would never say that this crazy woman was a world class curator.

‘Oh, helvete!’ she whispered when the Houses of Parliament and Big Ben appeared on the other side of the river.

‘Look to the right,’ Tony pointed at the giant Ferris wheel. ‘That’s the London Eye. I’m sure Professor Wright will give you a tour at some point. Ask him to take you up there, the view over the city is stunning.’

At this moment Erica was so happy, that even when she slipped her phone from the bag to check if there were any messages (and there were still none) she was able to keep the smile on her face and create the impression that she wasn’t disappointed. *I am perfectly fine.*

She felt different. On adventure, on a mission. She just wasn’t as bothered as she usually would be by the fact that even though it had been only a few hours since she has left, but she was still expecting just a quick check from back home on how her journey was. She knew that Granny and technology were not the best relationship, so it might take a while to hear from her, (and Erica would most likely just have to make this phone call herself), but from Bjørn? She tried her best not to overthink it. Right now, in her head it wasn't that he was clearly not as interested as she thought, he was just busy. So busy that he didn't have a few freaking seconds to just make sure that she got to London safe and sound. Huh!

Her thoughts were interrupted by Tony announcing they had arrived at her hotel in Bloomsbury. She thanked him, got out the car, put her bag on the ground and had a quick look at the place. She wanted to make sure that indeed it was a hotel. It looked like an ordinary Georgian house, especially with houses to its right and left looking very similar. All symmetric and proportional.

The building was white and had three storeys. Rooms on the first floor had access to a pretty balcony. Erica smiled back at Tony who nodded then drove off. She saw on one of the two entrance pillars a large black number '90'. She climbed the three steps and was about to knock on the door when she noticed a small sign, saying:

Welcome to the Blossom Inn. Please, ring the bell.

She rang the bell and entered.

Inside, a nice middle-aged receptionist with red hair and a pair of reading glasses hanging round her neck informed her that the room had been already paid for. She gave her a piece of paper with a message left for her this morning. Erica put it in her pocket and looked around. On the ground floor apart from the small reception area, there was a cosy living room with a fireplace, lots of books and board games, sofa and TV. At the back, a table for six people and in the corner an area to make tea or coffee. There were jars of biscuits too. Around was this indescribable atmosphere of old house, but at the same time it was very clean with modern accents. Not the cheapest but not the most expensive either.

After a quick glance around the place, Erica wanted to go straight to her room. She grabbed the key from receptionist. It was attached to a metal medallion with a big No. 1 on it, and she immediately felt a pleasant cold. It was so hot outside and not any better in the hallway, that holding the little piece of metal brought some small relief. She picked up her bag and turned to the stairs. At the bottom step she noticed her shoelace was untied and as her hands were both busy holding a bag, her coat and the key, she decided to fix it later. She was only going to the first floor.

Erica looked up, quickly counted the steps in front of her and thought, *what can happen? There's only twenty-five of them.* She started to climb the wooden staircase. It was painted in white to match all other little details of the hallway. The stairs were half-carpeted in navy and above each step were pictures which showed the day-to-day London life of Georgian times. Erica loved this kind of thing. She was looking at them so closely, she wasn't paying any attention to where she was going. She was halfway up the stairs when she tripped, sprawling her things all around. She quickly looked around. *Maybe no one saw it* she thought. She quickly rubbed her hands on her thighs, picked up her stuff, and using her long legs darted upstairs like a startled fawn. A hot wave went through her body. So hot, that this time even a cold piece of metal she still held in her hand, couldn't help her. She unlocked the door and, like the same fawn, bolted inside.

Erica disappeared behind the door with number 1. Some people could say that she was clumsy, she liked to think that it was because of laziness. Of course, it wasn't because she just missed a step, it was because she was too lazy to tie her shoelace. Her room was on right by the staircase. When she opened the door, she immediately realised that this is the lucky room with the balcony. She went outside and admired the view over the park. Tall green trees, people sitting on the grass having late lunch, dogs running around. Everybody was clearly enjoying the nice weather. When she got back inside and closed the door, she noticed that the windows must have been very thick, as no car or any other noises were heard.

She looked around her room. The place wasn't big but it had a private bathroom, which was enough for her. She wasn't a fussy person. As long there were basics provided, she was happy. The first thing most people usually do when they arrive in new place is to unpack, but Erica wasn't really the type of woman who would worry if her T-shirt was wrinkled and besides, she didn't really have much to unpack anyway.

She put her hands into her trouser pockets and found the note receptionist gave her when she checked in. She opened out piece of paper and read:

> Welcome to London, Doctor Skyberg!
>
> Thank you very much for such a prompt arrival.
>
> Unfortunately, an important meeting came up and I was unable to greet you at the airport. Please accept my apologies and thank you for your patience.
>
> I will see you shortly.
>
> Kind Regards,
>
> *Prof. R. Wright*

‘Seriously?’ she said out loud. ‘That's it? *I will see you shortly?’*

She sat on the bed and turned on the TV. She chose the BBC in the hope there might be more information regarding the recent events at the British Museum. But no luck. Politics, a long cover story about climate change and the ongoing big protest in central London, some drama on the Royal Family. But nothing about the robbery or the security guard’s killers. She turned the TV off and sat for a moment in silence wondering if she could leave the hotel. Professor Wright never mentioned, when he’d contact her, whether he was just going to show up here, if he was going to ring her first or if they were still even meeting today at all. Erica didn't like it. As much as she looked to other people as disorganised and a bit chaotic, and as much as she would overthink everything, this situation really annoyed her.

For Odin's sake she thought, *This is my very first time outside of Norway. I am not going to be sitting here like a little girl waiting for instructions from some man I don’t even know. And when all’s said and done, I am doing him a favour coming here, so if he wants to, he can find me.* She caught her reflection in the mirror – tired but confident. *That’s settled then. I will.* At that moment her phone rang.

'Hi honey, it's me.’

‘Hi, Gran,’ Erica smiled. Good old Gran. ‘Everything alright?’

‘Yes, yes, I am just checking if you got to your hotel safely. How was the flight?’ Her voice was faint and Erica realised she missed her.

‘I’m fine, everything’s good. I got here not that long time ago. Very nice place. The flight was okay.’

‘Oh, I am glad,’ her gran said with a cheery voice. ‘Right, I won’t take more of your precious time, honey. And knowing you, you were just about to go out and explore.’

‘Oh, Granny, you know me so well! I can’t hide anything from you!’ She liked how true that was, how close they were.

‘Enjoy, speak to you soon!’ and Granny Greta hung up.

Erica held her phone close to her chest and took a moment to think about her grandmother. Yes, they were very close. Erica’s mum had died giving birth to her, her dad ran away after that, and then it was just the two of them. She didn't have any other family. Since she could remember, Granny was always there for her. They really didn’t have any secrets. If she failed an exam, if some boy broke her heart, whatever it was, Granny Greta would always find some kind words to cheer her up. Erica knew she could always rely on her. She was the one person whose judgement and advice she really trusted. She knew it was corny, but they had this special bond that nothing could ever destroy. Yes, she’d go out and tell Gran all about it later.

After a quick shower, Erica changed her clothes for something a little bit lighter, more appropriate for the sunny weather. She swapped her boots for Vans trainers, put her valuables in the belt bag which she slung over her shoulder and hung her small Canon camera around her neck. She felt ready to be the perfect tourist, except for one thing. She had no clue where to go!

Erica came down the stairs, carefully watching every move she made, especially paying attention on the step she stumbled on just few hours ago, upon her arrival. *Classic me* it crossed her mind. She came over to the reception desk, where overly cheerful receptionist greeted her again.

‘Hello Miss Skyberg, is everything alright? How can I help?’ she put away the papers she held and stood upright in front of her guest.

Dr Erica Skyberg took an instant liking to the woman and let the ‘Miss’ slide. ‘Hello, yes,’ she said. ‘You see, this is my very first time in London and I don’t know much about the city. Would you be able to recommend anything to me?’

‘Absolutely!’ the receptionist smiled as if she had just been waiting for an opportunity to feel useful. She left the counter and with a hand gesture encouraged Erica to follow her. On the other side of the room, in the corner, was a small wooden stand with colourful brochures.

‘Oh, this is so exciting!’ she said. ‘I remember when I came to London for the very first time, and as you can see, my dear, I loved it so much I never left!’

Erica laughed. She started to go over the flyers, reading each attraction’s name out loud, ‘London Eye, Madame Tussauds, National History Museum, Royal Albert Hall, Hop On, Hop Off bus.’

‘My favourite!’ the receptionist interjected. She couldn’t hide the excitement. ‘The number one attraction I always recommend to our guests is the Hop On, Hop Off bus. I’ve done it dozens of times. It gives you the best opportunity to see London’s major landmarks with just one bus ride!’

‘Just one?’

‘Yes!’

‘Sounds good, any tips on where I should start?’ asked Erica staring at the many bus routes.

‘London Bridge, my dear. Take the Central, that’s the red line, from Tottenham Court Road to Bank. There you will change to the Northern line – the black line – for one stop. You can start exploring the city from the beautiful Tower Bridge, only short walk from the station, then cross the river to visit the magnificent Tower of London and then hop on,’ she paused to enjoy the pun, ‘the bus to discover rest of the city.’

Her enthusiasm was catching. ‘That is amazing, thank you! Do you know where I can get a ticket?’ said Erica, folding the map.

‘You can buy a temporary Oyster card at the Tube station and the Hop On, Hop Off ticket at any bus stop on this map. You will see guides in uniforms selling them and providing more information.’

Erica thanked the nice lady again and was just about to leave when she added, 'Oh, one more thing. If anybody phones or comes by looking for me, can you please tell them that I'm out, but they can reach me on my mobile?' The receptionist nodded with approval as Erica left the hotel.

She stopped right outside the main door. The hot air hit her face. She quickly entered the directions onto Google maps and followed the instructions. Tottenham Court Road station was indeed not far at all. Erica decided to take the kind lady's advice and did exactly what she said. She took the train and went to London Bridge. She was fascinated by everything. People in a rush, some rude, some polite, tourists standing on the wrong side of the escalator driving all the Londoners in a hurry crazy. There were talented buskers, like Tobias back home, entertaining the commuters. Everything was so different to life in Oslo. The number of different languages in such a small space amazed her. People from every part of the world. Some of them tourists like her, some of them who had managed to make a home here.

By the number of people getting in and out of London Bridge station, she guessed it was around 4 p.m. and everybody was leaving work for home. She looked up and noticed The Shard. Yes, she wanted to explore that area – she would change her plans! Then it occurred to her that although those Hop On buses sell tickets for 24 hours, they are not in fact in service for that length of time. She entered new directions into Google Maps. In a few minutes she was standing astonished in front of, she was sure, the most beautiful bridge she had ever seen. Maybe it was because of the heat or the fact she was abroad for the very first time and felt a little bit adventurous, she didn't really know, but she took a quick selfie to send to Granny and Bjørn. Gran Greta's answer came within seconds – 💕 And from Bjørn? Absolutely nothing. She grunted at his non-answer and crossed the River Thames. She found the bus stop, just like she was advised in the hotel. A man was selling tickets.

'Excuse me, how much is it?'

He looked at her and winked. 'It's £40, love, but I can sell it for the online price of £34.'

'Oh.' Erica was pleased at the bargain. 'Alright, but I have to choose only one route, is that correct?'

He winked again and smiled this time, 'For you, I will include all the routes and even chuck the river cruise for free!'

'Really?' *Londoners are so amazing*, she thought. 'How kind of you!' she said.

'Where are you from, darling?' the man asked, printing off the long ticket.

'From Norway.'

'Oh Norway, beautiful country,' he smiled, then continued: 'So, you can take this bus right here' – he pointed behind him – 'or go back to the Tower Pier and get a ferry to Westminster.'

'What would you recommend?' asked Erica not knowing what to do.

'River Cruise. On board there will be a tour guide explaining every landmark passing by and giving you all the fun facts, too. Then, you can take the bus leaving from just outside the Big Ben and continue your journey around the city. Hop On, Hop Off, see?'

The guy seemed lovely, trustworthy and sensible. Erica thanked him, turned around and made her way to the Pier, exactly where he directed her. On her way, she made a stop to take pictures of the Beefeaters standing at the entrance to the Royal Palace, but then quickly grew anxious that the ferry might be already at the pier. She didn't know how often they came and she decided to not waste more time in one spot. Too much to see. She quickly made her way to the river, showed her ticket to the steward and boarded the ferry.

The weather was still lovely, so the majority of the seats on the upper deck were already taken by excited tourists, but she managed to find one more right at the back. She had good luck today. And she was even more pleasantly surprised when it turned out that the boat wasn't going to do the Thames usual trip – the bridge and then turn around like other boats – but was going straight towards Westminster. She smiled, turned her face out to the sun and enjoyed the weather and funny commentary from the guide. During the cruise, a tall white building at the end of the Millennium Bridge caught her eye. She quickly wrote a note in her phone 'St. Paul's Cathedral'? to check on it and remember to go back another time. She found London Eye fascinating too, and put that in her notes next to the Cathedral. The ferry was slowly turning and there to her right were the Houses of Parliament. They took her breath away.

The boat pulled into dock. She left the ferry and went to the other side of Westminster Bridge to take a couple of pictures. She passed by a suspiciously large number of armed policemen. *Is it typical for this part of the city?* She wondered. Then, she remembered cute guide's advice, came back and started to look for the bus stop to continue the journey. She quickly unfolded her the map and decided to follow yellow line passing by Westminster Abbey, Buckingham Palace and into the heart of the city – Trafalgar Square. So, where was that stop? She looked around – Blue Route bus, there. And the Yellow Route but wrong direction. She saw all the company's competitor buses, but not the one she wanted. Where was this bus!

Then something else caught her attention.

The main road going to the right of the Big Ben was closed. Orange barriers stood right in the middle of the street and guards only letting in what looked like specially licenced vehicles. *Aaaah, that would explain why no buses are going that direction* she thought, and came up closer to the guards.

'Excuse me, sir, am I allowed to go over there?' She pointed in direction of the route she wanted to take.

The guard followed her finger and said, 'Yes, of course, but I wouldn't advise it. Unless you're one of *them*.'

'One of who? What is going on?' said Erica.

'One of the activists. There's a climate change protest been going on for a few days now, don't you watch the news?' He gave her an unbelieving look. 'The whole of central London is closed, because they block every major street and sleep in tents right in the middle of them.'

'Oh,' said Erica. 'Sorry, I didn't know. Thank you.' She nodded once. What to do? She decided to board the first Yellow Route bus she saw. She sat on the comfortable upper deck and enjoyed the view of the giant wheel on the other side of the Thames. She checked her map to see where she was going and decided it might be actually for the best – the bus was heading via Waterloo Bridge towards Leicester Square, which, as it turned out, wasn't too far from the place she had anticipated going to. She counted the stops, memorised them, put the map back in the belt bag, and relaxed. She was just admiring the city's landscape through her camera lens when she realised that, if her calculations were right, she had reached her stop. She hopped off the bus and took out her phone again. The bus stop was empty. She was really confused. She saw a lot of police on scooters passing by and quite few buses stopping but nobody getting off. Google Maps said that she was about a 30-minute walk away from her destination. She crossed the street, but something wasn't right. She noticed another bus pulling over, so without hesitation she jumped on, asked the driver where he was going and after hearing 'Buckingham Palace', flashed the ticket at him and made her way to the upper deck again.

All the buses were being diverted because of the climate change protests. She looked at her map and realised they were not really following their route, so she ended up on a bus going south instead of north of the river. She laughed out loud. She didn't mind it at all, she just wished that the very nice guide selling her the ticket, had mentioned possible disruptions. The bus rolled. At the stop another surprise.

'This bus terminates here, all change please,' said the driver. He politely asked all the passengers to leave the vehicle. Erica quickly realised where they were. She was going to go see Buckingham Palace. Outside the main gate she looked at it. It very much reminded her of the Royal Palace in Oslo. It was also at the end of a monumental road, with statues right in front of it. The pillars, the balcony, the colour of the front facade, everything very similar, apart from the guards. Here they were in their red uniforms and very recognisable black, hairy hats, the Union flag hanging proudly on the mast above the palace. It wasn't really something that interested Erica, so she decided to keep going. She still couldn't find any bus stop and now she was getting hungry. She Googled the nearest place to eat. By the time she'd found the pub and ordered some good English fish and chips, she realised that there was no more Hop On, Hop Off buses for today. She checked her map again. She was just a few meters away from Trafalgar Square.

Great she laughed out loud, *so I've just spent thirty something pounds for literally a two-stop bus ride!* She shook her head and kept smiling. This kind of thing happened to her all the time. In fact, this exact thing, messing up on a guided tour bus, happened when Matilde's friends were visited her in Oslo. They wanted to show them around but the buses ran only one or two stops. *What are the chances?* She said to the air. *I must be cursed or something! But that was okay.* On her way to Trafalgar, she took more pictures (of the protesters, the buildings, the streets) to make up for it.

Erica was fascinated by London, so much that she completely lost track of time. She hated to take photos with her phone so she hadn't checked the time in a while. After history, photography was probably her next favourite thing. She preferred to carry her small Canon camera with her, documenting everything around. She did that at home in Oslo too. When she wanted to get closer to nature or observe human behaviour it was perfect. She just loved to capture moments. Moments that at first might seem to disappear but then when the photos were developed, like history, they could last forever.

She clicked another photo. It started to rain, and it was getting dark. Erica didn't mind. Even though she didn't have any long sleeves or an umbrella, the air was still warm. She had wandered into the very vibrant China Town, and was just about to explore Soho, when a pedestrian nodded to her. She smiled at him. He nodded again and said:

'Your pocket's ringing, sweetheart.' He walked on.

'Oh? Oh,' Erica fumbled to quickly get the phone out. 'Thank you!' she called to the man. By the time she got to the phone, the ringing stopped. The caller left a voicemail.

'Hello, Doctor Skyberg? Yes, Professor Wright here. Apologies again for not picking you up from the airport. I hope you had a pleasant journey. I do realize that it is quite late, but I had hoped that we could still meet tonight. There is a pub a short walking distance from your hotel. I will meet you there at half past nine.' And the message ended. *That's it?* thought Erica. She was starting to get used to the Professor's very short messages but they were still irritating. Always just few short sentences. She looked at the time on her phone.

It was already nine o'clock.

Then she looked down at herself. Soaking wet. She would just have time to go back to hotel and change – it wasn't too far – and she simply couldn't imagine meeting Roger for the very first time looking like she just been swimming in the Thames in her clothes. She set off at a fast pace.

It didn't take her long to dry off, change and put on a bit of makeup. Just before she left her hotel once again that day, she quickly Googled 'The Red Lion'. It was the most common pub name in England! She hoped she'd got the right one.

And now she was repeating directions in her head *'left, right, left and then left again'*.

Luckily for her, the pub really was just around the corner. She wasn't sure how much further she can run. The cosy light from the pub had attracted quite a few people in this weather and pitch-dark neighbourhood. Even from a distance, passers-by were able to hear the loud, cheerful music and laughter.

Erica walked in, took off her hood and looked around. A friendly guy from behind the bar greeted her:

'Evening. Table at the far end, love.'

For English people, this was probably just an ordinary pub, nothing special, but Erica had never seen anything like it before: the bar was an island in the middle surrounded by tables in their own little sections and creating a very intimate atmosphere. In each section there was only two tables and few chairs. The windows weren't ordinary either, with their thick glass and lots of different patterns, so it wasn't possible to see what is going on inside. Anything could be happening. Secret meetings, love affairs…

Although they had never met in person before, somehow, they knew who they were looking for. Yes, she'd looked him up on the museum's website, but you can't always tell from the internet. Erica saw a man she knew in her heart to be Professor Wright, sitting at a table looking at his watch. He looked different than the website. More serious. Roger got up from his chair, shook her hand, quickly asked 'Beer?' and when she nodded her head with approval, went to the bar. Erica looked closely at her companion. He was young, tall, skinny but with a few muscles visible under his white shirt. His hair was brown and short, combed to the side, he also had a very short beard. Handsome, but not her type. It was the dark hair. She wasn't really sure if it was because the majority of Scandinavians were fair but blond guys were definitely who she liked. Like Bjørn. It had been nearly a whole day without any message from him. Her thoughts wandered to her Wednesday Guy. She'd been waiting for so long to talk to him, she decided she'd be the first to text him.

'IPA okay?' came a voice pulling her out of her thoughts of Bjørn. Roger put two pints of beer on the table. Erica tried to focus on him not her phone.

'Erm…?' Before she even managed to ask anything, Roger sat down and said:

'Apologies for such a weird way of contacting you. I just have to be exceptionally careful right now.' He hesitated for a second and took a sip of his drink. 'With the information in my possession I just need to be sure I can trust you.'

'What?' Erica couldn't lie. She was slightly terrified but intrigued at the same time.

'Look, I really don't have time to get to know you, but I need to know you'll be on my side. And that whatever you are about to hear or see it will stay just between the two of us.'

'What on earth are you talking about?' she said. *And what makes you think that I will be able to help?* she added to herself.

'It's the reason you're here.'

'The robbery?'

Roger nodded quickly. Erica stared at him.

'Quick question,' she said. 'Why not just talk to me on my mobile phone?'

'Ah, Scotland Yard. That Detective O'Sullivan. He suspects that I am not telling the entire truth. He thinks I'm hiding something. That maybe even it was me who stole the ring. I thought this way might be safer.'

'And? Is he right?' She couldn't help herself. She quickly looked at her phone again for anything from home.

Roger looked suspicious. 'Is everything okay? Are you waiting for a message?'

'Nothing important.' She put the phone back in her bag. 'So? This detective, Professor, is he right?'

‘Kind of. I mean, yes, he is.’ The Professor hesitated for a second ‘You see, Miss Skyberg,’ he lowered his voice and brought his face closer, ‘I have information that the ring that was stolen wasn’t real.’

Erica started choking on her beer. ‘Excuse me, what did you just say?’

‘The stolen ring. I believe it wasn’t real all along.’

Erica was confused. ‘Is this some kind of not-funny joke?’ she said.

‘Erm… no,’ said Roger.

‘Or maybe it’s funny but I just don’t get it? Is this what you call English humour?’ Erica was suddenly angry. Had he brought her here for nothing? She hesitated for a split second and then without saying a thing, grabbed her jacket from the back of her seat and stormed out. She was in such a rush that she didn’t even close the door behind her. *How dare he! I know I might not look like one, but I am a very respected academic in my country! The ring isn’t real? Was he really thinking he could fool me? Oh no, my dear, oh no.* Cold air hit her face. It wasn’t raining anymore, but everything still glistened. She heard Roger shouting after her, but she had no intention to stop at all. And if not for the fact that she really hated running, she would have disappeared before he could catch up to her.

‘Erica, wait! Let me explain!’

‘What is it to explain?’ she suddenly stopped. ‘What kind of nonsense you will try to sell me this time? You bring me here to this country, for what?’ They stood right in the middle of the street.

‘No, but you don’t understand…’

‘No,’ she interjected him, ‘I don’t. Tell me why you brought me here. Maybe the policeman is correct. You know that the ring isn’t real because you’ve stolen it and now, for some reason, want to involve me in this crime as well?’ She was talking so fast that Roger couldn’t even interrupt her. ‘I am a good person, Professor, a good person. I have never stolen, I have never hurt anybody deliberately, I do what the law says, and I don’t lie. I hate when something is unfair, and I hate seeing people do nasty things to other human beings.' All she could think about was the poor guard at the museum. Tears started running down her cheeks, she wiped them with end of her sleeve, turned around and walked away. She turned back abruptly. 'Why did you even want me here?' she snapped.

'The ring isn't real,' repeated Roger in a very calm voice, as if this would make Erica understand. 'I received a letter from my great-grandfather telling me that.'

'So? It doesn't mean it's true. And anyway, if it is, that would mean – Oh, Holy Odin!' She covered her mouth.

'Yes, that would mean that Einarr's treasure is still here in London,' said Roger. 'And I want you to help me find it'

'Me? But?' She stared at him, not sure. 'This letter, how can we know it is real?'

'That is why I need your help and expertise. There are some runic inscriptions I don't understand.'

Erica was curious. 'Do you have it? Can I see it?'

'No. With the theft and the murder, I don't want to risk it and carry it with me. Tomorrow night. Meet me at my house.'

'Your house?'

'Yes.'

Erica knew that the possibility to be involved in such an adventure might never come again. To find a treasure. A real Viking treasure. To have the chance to discover something her people left behind. To be a part of a historical moment and discover more about her ancestors. She stared at the professor. She could take this as a joke and go back home now or stay another 24 hours and see what happens.

Hhhnnhhhnnnn! An oncoming car honked its horn and snatched her out of her thoughts. She jumped back and turned on Roger.

'Twenty-four hours, Professor. That's all you have!' She spun around and went straight to the hotel without looking back.

Chapter 9

The olive-green Jeep parked outside the giant neoclassical building on the Great Russell Street, turned off its lights and acted like nobody was inside as if a ghost driver had driven it there. The sky thundered and a few bolts flashed just above the museum's roof. The rain was so heavy and so sudden that all the pedestrians nearby ran as fast as they could, as if their lives depended on it. It was only early evening, and still hot, but because of the weather it was already pitch black with the short exceptions of a bolt piercing the sky.

After nearly an hour spent in the car, the driver decided to leave the vehicle. It was like he had all the sudden realised that the rain wouldn't stop any time soon. He ran to the other side of the street, covering his body with the oversized raincoat and trying to protect his face and head from getting wet.

'Crazy weather, huh?' shouted the guard in his direction from little booth, his voice trying to beat the rain and wind.

'What?' the man shouted back.

'I said, crazy weather, huh? What on earth are you doing here at this time?' The guard opened the gate and seeing visitor's eyes set on his chest added, bragging a little, 'Bulletproof. Latest addition to our uniforms.' He pulled the vest a little bit out so the visitor could see better.

'Nice! I'm here just to fetch something! For Wright. Won't be long,' the huddled figure shouted back then disappeared behind the 'employees only' sign.

Chapter 10

Erica was wide awake, as she couldn't sleep at all. She thought over and over about what the professor had told her last evening. She wondered if she did the right thing. Shouldn't she call the police? Tell someone about it? If what Roger said was true, then everybody was looking for a fake ring? And a man had been killed for it. Would she go to jail for hiding information? She was lying in the bed, covered head to toe in the white fluffy duvet. Staring at the celling. When the morning alarm went on, she slowly switched it off, opened the curtains and grabbed her phone.

Two messages. First from Roger asking her to meet him at the British Museum at 10 o'clock today – so not at his home then? – she wondered. And the second message was from Bjørn. *That's a surprise,* she thought, smiling, and opened the text.

> *Hi Erica! So sorry for not writing before! I had a family event and have been busy. Hope the journey wasn't too bad and that London treats you well!*

Erica smiled and frankly speaking felt relief. Relief that she was not crazy and there was indeed something between the two of them. She had been hurt so many times in her life and was so lonely and unlucky in love so far, that she misjudged any signals very easily.

She automatically pressed the reply button, hesitated for a second, wrote a message and just before hitting 'send' hesitated again. *'Is it too soon? Won't I look too eager? Desperate? Helvete, always the same!'* She sat down back on the bed, throwing her phone on the pillow. She stared at it then turned on the TV. The weather forecast was showing another sunny week ahead, with showers during the night, even though it was already September and the weather should start to cool down at this time of the year. Her thoughts came back to Bjørn. She picked up the phone again and reminded herself of what Matilde told her not long ago: '*Erica, if you can't play fucking games, don't play them. If you want to text him, text him. If you want to see him, ask him out. Just do it.*' Her thumbs got to work.

Hi Bjørn! Yeah, London so far is good! 😊 *Have already met few people. What are you up to?*

This time the reply came so quickly she was glad she'd messaged back.

Few people, huh? Should I be jealous? 😊

'*Jealous? He's jealous!*' Erica was screaming in her head with excitement.

No need 😊 *What are your plans for the weekend?*

He didn't reply immediately as he did to the previous message. She put the phone down on the bed and went to the bathroom to get ready.

The nice receptionist greeted Erica downstairs. She informed her that there were fresh pastries next to the refreshments. As it was still early, she made a cup of coffee, grabbed a croissant and opened a newspaper which was lying on the table.

'Politics, politics, is this the only subject that Brits are talking about?' she murmured. But then a couple of pages later she came across a small article about the theft. They not only still didn’t have any suspects, but it got worse. Now the CCTV footage from that night was gone.

Chapter 11

Erica stopped right outside the British Museum. She was amazed by the size of the building. Compared to the Vikingship Museum it was enormous. She took a deep breath and for a split second wanted to turn around and even though she hated running, run. She wanted to escape. She knew she promised Roger to give him 24 hours to explain everything, but she still wasn't feeling comfortable with that situation. Why he couldn't explain it yesterday she didn't know. Except, of course, she ran off. But that was only natural – she didn't want to be a part of it, and yet… she just had this feeling in her gut that it would be worth it to stay. To give him a chance.

She walked in through the empty hall and reached the marble staircase. The museum had just been re-opened, so not many people were yet around. She stopped right in front of the stairs. She recognized them from the television and from the pictures in the paper. The lonely yellow 'Caution, wet floor' sign made the place look completely normal, as there had been no murder in that spot just a few days before. Erica stood there for few minutes, turning around, trying to picture what has happened that night. She wanted to understand the motive for killing the guard.

Roger swears he had nothing to do with it, she thought, *but is he covering for this killer? He could have knocked the guard down or shot him in the foot so he wouldn't follow him. Anything else but killing.* The whole thing made Erica uneasy.

She checked her watch. There was no sign of the professor. She decided to make her way upstairs. She wanted to see medieval section, mainly because this wasn't ever shown in the paper. There, in section 41, Erica entered the greatest collection of Anglo-Saxon objects in the world and the little less impressive – but still quite big – Viking section. She looked around, carefully examined each piece. She started to wonder why thieves were interested in that particular ring. That was the question that she didn't think to ask Roger yesterday. She was too shocked, so it slipped her mind. She'd have another chance. There were so many objects that surely were worth more.

In the middle of the room there was an empty cabinet with what it looked like a brand-new front window. Erica came a bit closer. There was a picture of a man called Sir Roger Wright in the corner and a small description of both the ring and discovery itself. The face of the man looked a little familiar. *Wait a minute,* Erica thought, a little shocked, *Sir Roger Wright?* The slip of paper said that the ring was cursed, but it didn't give any more details about the saga than Erica already knew. In fact, after reading this very short story, she felt like an expert. For the first time, she believed that she would be actually able to help.

'Ah, here you are. Good morning, Dr Skyberg, apologies for the wait,' Professor Wright said walking into the gallery. 'Did you find anything interesting?'

Erica looked at him and said, in a slightly snappy tone, 'As a matter of fact, yes I did find out something very interesting. Are you and the archaeologist who allegedly found the tomb, ehm,' she coughed for emphasis, 'related?

Roger smiled, thinly. 'Yes, Sir Roger was my great-grandfather. I have inherited his name.'

Erica stood staring at him and not saying anything. Through her head went so many different thoughts, that she just stood still a mix of emotions on her face. *So why on earth would he steal the ring if his own great-grandfather made the discovery?* she thought *AND why would he do that knowing that it is not Einarr's real ring? It's just doesn't make sense.*

The awkward silence was broken by an elderly gentleman who had just walked into the gallery. Chairman Applegate pointed towards the corner of the room and said in an apologetic tone, 'Excuse me, Professor Wright? Could I ask you to come here for just one moment?'

‘Oh, excellent timing, sir,’ said Roger. ‘I would like to introduce you to our special guest – the world class curator I told you about. She’s specializing in Vikings. Dr Erica Skyberg’ –he pointed one to the other – ‘this is Mr Applegate, the Chair of the museum’s Board of Governors.’

Erica came over to the two men. She still kept one eye on the display’s glass. She was clearly fascinated by the objects discovered in the tomb. She turned her head towards them, smiled and stretched her hand out to shake the chairman’s hand. The expression on his face couldn’t fool anyone. He was obviously surprised, shocked and not at all happy at who or rather what he was seeing. He looked at her from head to toes, paying special attention to the piercings on her face and the visible tattoos on her shoulders, uncovered between the tank top and loose jumper she was wearing. He thought that this was some kind of joke and the real curator hadn’t arrived yet. He thought the woman was too young to have such a position and knowledge, and definitely the person who stood in front of him didn’t look serious or mature enough. But he swallowed his pride and said, graciously:

‘Welcome to London, madam. Pleasure to have you here. Might we go to my office to have a chat?’ He gestured to the doorway and looked at Roger with eyes saying *What were you thinking?* Roger smiled at him, innocently.

It took several minutes to get to the other side of the building. Even by using the secret passages and shortcuts that the old man knew, it seemed to Erica that it was a long way. For her it wasn’t a big deal but watching the elderly Mr Applegate shuffling such a distance helped by his walking stick was breaking her heart. Upon arrival at his office, the chairman put the key into the lock, turned it and slightly opened the door. He gestured with his hand and said: ‘Ladies first.’ As soon as Erica stepped into his office, he quickly blocked the way for Roger.

'Actually, Professor,' he whispered, 'I don't think I need your help here' and without waiting for any response, he shut the door right in Roger's shocked face.

Chapter 12

Roger was staring at the door in front of him with his mouth slightly open, thinking *What the hell?* The door was so close to his face, that he could see the detail in its texture. He took a second to try to analyse what just happened. This is not how it meant to be. He was supposed to be there, inside, with them, listening and being a part of this conversation. After all, he was the one who brought Dr Skyberg here. He was the one with the plan and now he was scared that something might not go accordingly. What were they saying to one another? What was she telling the chairman? He was just thinking how much he'd already told her, when the door suddenly opened.

'Yes? Can I help you there?' asked the chairman. He was looking at Roger's fist still held in the air. 'Were you knocking?'

'Oh no, no I was just… emm… I was, I think I left my coat inside,' stuttered Roger, clearly surprised by his own actions as well. He had been so deep in his thoughts, that he himself hadn't noticed he'd knocked on the door.

'Professor, you haven't been inside my office today. I suggest you check your own, maybe it's over there,' he said in a polite manner. Then he shut the door again, only to open it just few seconds later. 'Professor, what is the matter with you! Are you eavesdropping?'

'What? No! No, how could I? What for? I am… I'm just going to the coffee shop, yes that's it, and I wanted to ask if you or Dr Skyberg would like a beverage?' he quickly lied. The chairman thought he saw a small red bruise on his colleague's forehead from banging it on the door while trying to hear their conversation.

'Did you sleep well today, my son? You know that I have coffee and a kettle in my office. I've made you many times a mug there. But I would strongly advise you go to your coffee shop and to grab yourself one. A strong one.' He pointed a finger at him which was suppose make this statement serious 'And wait to hear from us. This meeting might take a while.'

Clearly puzzled by his own behaviour, Roger stepped away and made his way to the café located on the museum's first floor, right by the entrance to the medieval section. He joined the queue minding his own business and trying to decide which one of all displayed delicious cakes he would get, when he overheard some of the staff members behind the counter whispering to each other:

'Apparently he was shot from this spot right here,' said a girl in a Polish accent who was making the coffee. She pointed with her eyes and chin at a little spot by the viewing point, just few feet away.

'I heard a rumour that it was an inside job!' whispered her colleague in a clear Australian accent, and turned around to serve another customer. 'Next please!'

Roger, curator in this institution, renowned professor but most importantly, Mike's colleague and friend, felt that the conversation between the girls was inappropriate. Regardless, if they were telling the truth or not. And if he could hear them, every other person in the queue could hear them as well. He looked over at where the girl had been talking about and it all came flooding back. Roger was certain that he would never, ever, forget the events of that night. He remembered them so well.

It was very late, way past midnight, when he got a call from Scotland Yard asking him to come to the museum as quickly as possible. They didn't go into any details, just informed him that the matter was serious. Roger was still awake because just a few hours earlier he had the unexpected visitor of the solicitor Mr Evans in his house. He had been reading over and over again the letter from his great-grandfather and was carefully studying the map trying to make any sense of it, when Detective Charlie O'Sullivan called. He quickly took a photo of the map – he didn't want to risk anything by carrying it with him – then hid it and the letter in a drawer, grabbed his coat and called for a cab. When he arrived at the museum, there was chaos. Lots of police cars in front of the main gate, helicopters patrolling from the sky, people in uniforms running around with dogs, clearly trying to find a trace of someone. He showed his pass and went inside where the Irish detective met him by the stairs.

'Good evening,' said O'Sullivan.

'Good evening,' said Roger. Then, without any chit-chat, they made their way up and the detective briefly told the curator what happened. When he finished, they were just passing by the spot where Mike had been shot. Roger came closer.

'Just don't touch anything!' the policeman shouted.

Roger carefully looked over the site and immediately regret it. He wasn't disgusted easily but he didn't expect to see Mike's body, which wasn't even covered yet because the coroner was still in the process of the investigation. Blood was everywhere. Roger knew that he would never forget this moment. He shuddered, quickly turned around and followed Detective O'Sullivan to the gallery, where Roger's colleague, Professor Cox was waiting for them.

'Yes sir, how can I help? Sir?' The Australian girl at the register tried pulled Roger's attention back to the present day 'Hello? There's a queue behind you!'

'Erm, a large black Americano and a slice of carrot cake, please,' he finally answered, slowly taking his sight away from the spot. He passed her his employee pass to get a staff discount.

'Oh, you are a curator here. I didn't know. I am sorry, sir,' said the girl in an apologetic manner, feeling ashamed of the way she spoke to him just a second ago.

'Clearly,' he said, sharply, taking his change. 'And find another topic to talk about at work, please.' The girl looked more embarrassed and said nothing in reply.

Roger walked away and put his tray down on one of the tables furthest away, carefully chosen to not be facing either the café or the viewpoint. He had to get his mind off this awful flashback. *The map* he thought and took his phone out of one of the pockets in his trousers. With the call from the police, the news about Mike, the ring and meeting with the Board, he hadn't had much time just yet to properly examine it. From the texture and look of it, he was guessing that it was drawn or more likely tattooed with ink on some animal's skin. *Maybe reindeer?* he thought. He took a bite of cake and continued flicking through the pictures on his phone, from time to time zooming in and out of parts of it.

What fascinated Roger was that it looked like it had two layers. The original map showing a very simple plan of what it looked like a village or a city, with definitely more details in the area just above the river, and some runic inscriptions. And then a second layer. Overlaid on top of the black ink were several different coloured lines, going in several different directions. On each line, every now and then, there was a dot and tiny caption right next to it. It was in modern English letters, not in runes. Roger zoomed in on one: 'Strand'. He zoomed out and zoomed in the right top corner of the picture. There was some kind of key of what each of the coloured lines meant.

Bakerloo, Central, District... Oh my god! This is the London Underground Map! But why? And Strand? There is no such a station, but... hey hey! I think there had been, there had been such a station! He looked closer. *This must be one of the first Tube maps ever drawn! But how on earth would my dear ancestor be in the possession of it?* Roger paused for a moment. His coffee grew cold as he carried on: *Unless... he did mention in his letter Mayor Anderson. As far as I know, he had a great impact on London's Tube growth. And my great-grandfather called him a close friend. But surely other people would have noticed and questioned their actions. Or, would they...? After all, they were a Knight of the Realm and the Mayor. But... would they be brave and cheeky enough, to manipulate the Queen herself and have the engineers to dig exactly where they thought the treasure could be?*

Giving them the impression that this was the best route to build tunnels for the London Underground trains? Is this why there are quite few disused stations that didn't make sense to be built in the first place? Because my great-grandfather thought Einarr could be buried over there? Roger smiled a little at this enterprise. *I wonder what all those runic inscriptions mean. They look Viking. I should probably get Erica to help me translate them.*

Erica! She's still with Chairman Applegate! Roger quickly looked up almost tipping his cup. *God, I hope she doesn't tell him too much. But then... what does she actually knows? She thinks I have dragged her all the way from Norway to help find real tomb and the treasure. And to help the officials find missing ring.* Roger glanced at the map again. *But she knows it's fake. Would she say something?*

Chapter 13

Erica sat down comfortably on one of the armchairs in front of the desk and started to feel a little bit intimidated by the fact that the chairman had decided to leave Roger out of this conversation. She wondered if the curator had in fact done something suspicious or bad. Was she the one who should somehow rat him out and get him into trouble? She knew that Roger lied to her and knew more about the ring than he initially told her. He had known for sure the ring was a fake, but then on the other hand, there could be simply more to it than she realised.

Mr Applegate sat down opposite her, entwined his hands, and put them on the desk. He stared at her in complete silence. She felt his eyes on her septum piercing, the parts of her body where her tattoos were visible and her platinum hair shaved neatly on one side of her head. She was used to people on public transport or on the street always looking at her. She didn't have problem with it. It just amused her that whenever she helped elderly ladies to cross the road or carry shopping bags because they looked heavy, or when she picked up something a stranger in front of her had just dropped, any small act of kindness and humanity, people always looked really surprised. As if her tough appearance never truly reflected what kind of person she is. Like every person with tattoos must have been to prison. She got used to it. But she was a little bit surprised that the chairman was doing exactly the same thing. She thought that in such diverse country as the UK nobody cared anymore, but maybe people were people everywhere. It was in Erica's nature to be friendly, so she smiled and broke the silence:

'Is everything alright, Mr Applegate?'

'Oh yes, yes, apologies, you just remind me my granddaughter Becky, but she is quite a troublemaker, so I guess I am just trying to get my head around that you are a world class curator.'

Erica blushed.

'Would you like a cup of tea, my darling?' he said and helping himself with his stick he tried to get up.

'I would love a cup of coffee, but allow me sir, please.' She got up and signalled him to sit back down. She put the kettle on a said 'By the way, I didn't have a chance yet to thank you for the invitation. I am not going to lie; I was really surprised when I got a call from Professor Wright.'

'And why is that if I may ask?'

'I guess, I just don't know how I might help. I am neither a detective nor a policeman, but I am guessing that is why we are having this meeting, am I right, sir?' she said putting two mugs on the desk.

'Yes, that is correct. Can I just ask you first, when exactly did you get call from Roger and what did he say or promise, perhaps?'

Strange question, thought Erica, but she said: 'Let me think.' She stopped for a moment. 'He called on Thursday, two days ago, very early morning. He asked me to turn on the BBC where the press conference from the museum was being transmitted. He didn't give me any details, just asked if I could come over to London the next day. He said that my flight and hotel have been paid for. And I think that's it. I just assumed that he needs my expertise as the stolen object belonged to the Vikings and I know a thing or two about them,' she smiled modestly.

The chairman didn't say anything at first, trying to figure if what she just said made sense and coincided with Roger's version.

'So, what can you tell me about the ring and the saga. We think that the theft was connected with its origin but the Einarr Saga is not particularly popular or well-known over here. Maybe it was years ago, as hidden treasure gives it a little bit mystery – and if it had been lost forever, people might be still interested in more research – but as you know the tomb was found and the treasure put on display here. So people took interest in other sagas. Now, with the ring as the only item from the exhibition missing, it gets us here Miss– sorry Dr Skyberg. So, why? What was so special about it?'

Erica smiled, finished her coffee, closed her eyes and began to recite in her soft Norwegian voice:

When Einarr was brought into this world, he did not know how strong the significance of his name would be. That 'Lonely Warrior' would destine him to be the greatest Viking hero Norway had ever seen. But also, that he would die alone.

At a very young age, Einarr was orphaned. The family of his closest friend took him in and raised him with their son, Audun. The two were inseparable as brothers.

Einarr was known for being a warrior with great fighting skills, compassion and a kind heart. It was not long before the King's daughter, Princess Ingrid, and Einarr, fell in love. One day, upon hearing that the very powerful Völva named Hertha, had returned to the local woods, Audun asked his brother to visit her with him. Audun wanted her to foresee the future for him. Using her runestones, the Norse shaman saw that he would indeed find a great love but also, that plague was coming to Norway and he would lose his life. This terrified Einarr's brother, but neither of the warriors would show their fear.

One year to the day, the King of Vikings decided to invade England. Einarr knew the expedition could take years, and desired to marry Princess Ingrid before he left his beloved country. In the village, he found the best craftsmen who learned their skills from dwarfs themselves and bade them to make the two most beautiful rings anyone had ever set eyes on. They went to the temple. At its centre was a runestone made to honour the marriage of Odin & Freya. The craftsmen cut out two pieces from the stone and on each engraved the Viking symbol of man and woman. Combined they made up the symbol of love:

And Einarr was happy.

With the rings in his hand, he remembered Hertha's prophecy about the plague. He travelled back into the woods to ask Völva to cast a spell on the rings: whosoever owns them, will be protected against all disease.

Hertha added two precious gemstones to each symbol on the ring. "Now, my lord," she said, "I have gifted you with the symbol of family:

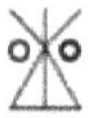

"The gemstones will change colour every time you and your Beloved think of each other."

With three days until the expedition, Einarr proposed to his love. Ingrid rejected him. Her heart, she said, belonged to his brother, Audun.

For a third time, Einarr returned to the Norse shaman. This time heartbroken and bereft. When he spoke, his voice was low and long: "Curse this ring. Curse it with loneliness forever."

"And then?" asked Völva.

"Then I will trick my brother to take it. And when he proposes to my Ingrid, she will fall under the curse and be forever lonely and not capable of love."

"Are you sure?" asked Hertha.

"I am," said the warrior.

But he was not sure. On his way back to the village, Einarr had a change of heart. His pain was such that he never wanted to fall in love again. The lonely warrior kept the cursed ring for himself. He would be incapable of love.

Even in his grief, he remembered the shaman's warning. Plague was coming to Norway. Although he had no love for any woman, he still had love for his brother. He gave the blessed ring to Audun, to be protected by spell.

When Einarr was leaving this world, even though he was far away from home, he was surrounded by his brothers. They left with the 'Lonely Warrior' gifts for their Gods, hoping that when he enters Valhalla, they will receive them and help all Vikings to win their battles.

Upon return to his beloved Norway, Audun quickly realised that Hertha's prophecy was fulfilled. Plague had ravaged the surrounding villages and many people died. His Ingrid died. Audun had wished to go to Valhalla but on hearing of Ingrid's death, he killed himself to join his beloved in the afterlife.

Erica finished and opened her eyes. Chairman Applegate was clearly impressed.

'Now, that was something, my child. That was something. I thought you would tell me few short sentences, but this? I wish I'd recorded it. Well, when we find the ring, I would love to put the whole saga right next to it.'

Erica smiled. 'No problem, Chairman Applegate. I can write it down and email it to you' she said knowing that this will make him happy.

'Really? That would be wonderful!' he beamed and gave her his business card.

'Can I be any more help?'

'No, no dear, you have done enough. I think you had better go and find Roger.'

She stood up, shook his hand by way of a goodbye and left Mr Applegate's office.

Chapter 14

In the hallway there was no sign of Roger. Fair enough. Nobody knew how long the meeting would last. Erica grabbed her phone from her pocket and was pleasantly surprised. *Three messages! I am on fire today!*

First – from Bjørn:

> Not much to be honest. Will probably hang in the bar. Wish you were here! How are things going?

Second – from Gran Greta:

> Just checking if everything is okay honey. Love you. Granny.

Third – from Roger:

> I am waiting in the café on the first floor. Once you finish, please come and find me.

It sounded like his usual curt messages.

After taking a few wrong turns, Erica managed to find the right coffee shop.

'Do you know how many cafés are on the first floor?' she said with sarcasm and sat down opposite the professor.

He quickly turned off his phone in a little panic and put some notes into his pocket. She looked at him and thought *that's a little bit odd* but decided to not say anything; it wasn't her business and it was clear it wasn't something he wanted to share. He obviously wanted to hide it from her. She quickly came to the conclusion that, if he would be willing to, then he would show it to her. Nagging someone to do something they didn't want to wasn't really her style.

‘Hello! How did it go?’ Roger asked her.

‘I must say, Chairman Applegate is a decent guy,’ she smiled.

Roger glanced at her and, with caring voice, asked: ‘Are you hungry? Would you like to grab some lunch?’

‘Actually, if you don’t mind, I would like to have another look at the display,’ she politely rejected his proposition and pointed over at the door with the sign ‘Medieval Section’ above its entrance.

As soon as they walked into the gallery, Roger let his guest explore the room, all the while watching Erica’s every move very closely. He was curious what would catch her attention first. If there was anything that she had never seen before – that they don’t have at the Vikingship Museum perhaps? He wondered if his museum might be in possession of some unique artefacts that would make even her really impressed? He didn’t know why but he liked the thought of that.

Erica didn’t take long to look around, but one particular display drew her attention.

‘Wow!’ she gasped with excitement and hurried to one side of the gallery. ‘Is this? Are those the artefacts from Einarr’s tomb?’ She touched the glass, lovingly. ‘Allegedly, I mean.’

‘Yes, indeed they are – eh? What–’ Roger stopped in the middle of the sentence. He had been so busy focusing on the matter that the stolen ring was fake, that he hadn’t even thought that rest of the discovered objects were fake as well. For a second he started to question authenticity of every single item on that display, but quickly realised, they all were found in a Viking tomb. True, it wasn’t Einarr’s tomb, but it did belong to a Viking.

Then his mind started to wonder… *‘Why that ring? What is it so special about it? There is so many beautiful objects here or other rings in other displays. Why that one? And it happened on the night when I got the letter? Isn’t that too much of coincidence?’* Then he thought: *‘No it must be. If the thieves knew about the letter, they would have known that the ring is also fake. It's a coincidence–'*

'Are you kidding me?' Erica squealed. She made Roger jump as she raised her voice and looked at him with the biggest smile. 'We also have a Vegvisir in our collection but this one? *Bare fantastisk!*' She stared in wonder at the object in front of her.

'Excuse me, what did you just say?' Roger for a split second thought he had a problem with his hearing.

'Vegvisir, the Viking Compass. We have one. It was discovered on the Oseberg Ship in 1904, but believe me, ours is not as nice as yours!'

'Vegvisir? What do you mean? Vegvisir is an object not a person? And there's more than one kind?' asked Roger. With curiosity he remembered the last line of the letter from his great-grandfather. His heart started beating faster and faster.

'Why would it be a person? Where did you get that idea from, Professor, huh? Of course it is an object, and of course there are different kinds. They all very similar and they all represent the symbol of Protection and Guidance.' Her eyes were twinkling. 'Each of them contains eight staves, you see? Do you know that the word *Vegvisir* means literally "wayfinder" *and* "signpost"?'

'No, no I didn't,' said Roger. Then, hoping he would find out what his great-grandfather meant by this object being a key to the map, he asked, 'What else can you tell me about it?'

'Well, it has never been confirmed in terms of real history, but it is mentioned in two ancient manuscripts: *The Huld* and *The Galdrabok*. As the Galdrabok is considered to be a textbook for magic, people believe that Vegvisir has special powers. Do you want to know the fun fact? According to that book, Vegvisir will provide guidance and protection, but in order to do that, it should be drawn in blood on a human's forehead. While the Huld says that just as long as you have it, you will arrive to your destination safely.'

Roger was impressed. 'I must say, Dr Skyberg, you have a very impressive knowledge of Vikings.'

Erica turned around with slight surprise but still smiling. 'Is it not the reason you brought me here?' she said. She turned back to the compass and whispered for only she and the compass to hear 'You are beautiful.' Then she said over her shoulder:

'Professor…' she started slowly. 'Do you think it would be possible to arrange for me to examine this compass a little bit closer? This is not like the one at the museum back home. Look, it has both cardinal and intercardinal points around it and this additional disc with runes on it.' She felt giddy. 'And not only Viking runes! This is an Old Futhark! An Old Futhark! What a treat!' She bit her knuckles to let go of some of the emotions.

'I believe, I could arrange it for you,' said Roger, selfishly thinking only about how this compass could help him to unlock the map.

***

Erica positioned herself comfortably on the hotel bed, getting ready for a quiet night with Chinese takeout, a few beers and a cheesy movie in English. When had she left the museum earlier, she had been messaging with Bjørn on the way back.

Erica – Pub? 🍻

Bjørn – No, changed my mind. Having a few friends over, will cook for them.

He was so nice. So, when he sent her a text apologising for the late reply to her last one, and telling her everyone had just left, she decided to not only call him but to FaceTime him instead. It had been a couple of days since she'd seen his face. Bjørn answered the video call surprisingly quickly. He looked exactly as she has remembered. Shoulder length blond hair, blue eyes behind round glasses, maybe a little cheeky but smile that made her heartbeat faster. His unbuttoned shirt showed his muscles and slightly tanned chest. He combed his hair with a hand and said:

'Hey Rick, what's going on?'

'Hi Bjørn, just wanted to check in. How was the dinner? And seriously, you cooked? I didn't know you have so many skills.'

'Yeah, they all just left, so I am cleaning up. But tell me, how is London treating you?'

'It's great! The city, people – well, the professor's a bit annoying but that's fine – the British Museum. They have so many artefacts I've never seen, so it's all very exciting,' she said with a happy smile. Then she heard a weird sound in the background of Bjørn's flat. 'Is everything okay? What's that running water noise? Have you left a tap on?' She pictured his kitchen sink overflowing…

'Oh yeah,' he answered in a mysterious voice. 'That's nothing, don't worry about it. Listen, I have to go, I will text you tomorrow.' He nervously looked around.

'Yes, sorry.' *That felt abrupt,* thought Erica. Then she added: 'I-I don't want to bother you, just wanted to see you,' and she was just about to end the video call when she saw something in the background. 'What was that?' She fell completely silent, then after a short moment sat straight up and nearly shouted: 'Was that Matilde just going into your bedroom wearing only a towel?'

Bjørn looked embarrassed, then said:

'Sorry Rick, that you had to find out this way, but yeah, I don't think we should be seeing each other anymore.'

'But - but you just said – wait, what? I don't understand.' She felt her eyes becoming watery. Not wanting to cry in front of him and to show that she didn't care anyway, she quickly added: 'I hope you both will be very happy.'

'Er–' Bjørn tried to stop her but she pressed the red button to finish the conversation.

She slammed her phone on the bed, grabbed the beer and blanket and went to sit on the balcony. She had to analyse this.

'What the hell has just happened?' All these mixed emotions, all so strong that she couldn't keep her thoughts inside her head. She was literally talking out loud to herself.

She sat on the chair, covered her legs with the blanket, took such a big sip of the beer, that the bottle was instantly half empty and started her monologue:

'Well done to me. Well done. How is it even possible? How on earth can a thirty-two-year-old woman not keep a guy for longer than a one-night stand? Is it something wrong with me? Have I done something? Or maybe haven't done enough? And *Matilde*. Maybe it would be easier to swallow if it had been someone I don't know. But *her*? I seriously thought that we were friends. I trusted her and confided to her. Ever since we met. I know that we haven't known each other for a crazy amount of time, but still, I never thought that any guy would be more important than our friendship.'

Erica finished the beer, went for another one and remembered how Matilde would tell the story of how the two of them met. Erica liked how Matilde told it from her point of view; it gave Erica some lovely details of what people thought when they met her for the very first time. And now, beer in hand, she closed her eyes and pictured Matilde, with her long ginger hair sitting next to her – as if she were her best friend – telling the story to new colleagues at work:

I was walking from the ferry stop on Bygdøy Island towards the museum. Then all the sudden, I noticed a wallet fall out of the pocket of someone in front of me. I picked it up and opened quickly. The girl smiling from the picture on the driver's licence was no further than 100 yards in front of me. Yes, it was you, Rick. I started to run and thought that it was funny, because you couldn't be really smiling on that picture, as it was an official photo, but there was something in your eyes that was telling me that you were.

'Hey!' – I started to shout, still running – 'Hey stop! Your wallet!' Random people started to turn around. Everybody but you, Rick. Remember, you had those big headphones on your head. You were listening to the music and simply didn't know what was going on around you. By now, we were in the parking lot leading to the main entrance, so I started to run faster, before you went inside and disappeared in the crowd.

'Heyyyy!' I finally caught up to you and tapped your shoulder. You took your headphones off and turned around. You looked worried. 'Are you okay?' you asked. I was panting. I'd been running for ages.

'I believe this belongs to you' I said in a weird voice, my throat sore. I stretched out my hand with your wallet. And then you thanked me without even checking if any money was missing, and you offered to show me around if I was going to the museum. And I said that I actually have a job interview over there, so you gave me some very useful tips and afterwards we went for that first beer together. And that is how our friendship started.

Erica opened her eyes, damp with held-back tears, and was back in Bloomsbury. She really liked this story. From the very moment she met Matilde, she'd trusted her instantly, thought they were close friends. Matilde knew how hard it was for Erica to like somebody, to express her feelings and tell someone other than her gran about it. Matilde also knew how rare it was that Erica kissed someone or spent a night with them. So, as her friend, Matilde should have known that this will really hurt her. Especially that all this time Erica was talking about 'Wednesday Guy' and Matilde gave her nothing but support. She could have mentioned she liked him as well. That might have been different.

And Bjørn? Of all the girls in the world it had to have been her friend. Erica felt stupid. She would have never done anything like that. She felt used and humiliated.

Embarrassed for being on the outside a strong woman but on the inside some fragile romantic who just wanted to be loved. The tears started running down her cheek. She felt sorry for herself – she just couldn't understand how on earth it was possible that she was a thirty-two years old and never been in a relationship. People her age were not only married by this time, some of them were already divorced!

Her stomach began to hurt now, so she squeezed it with both hands. Her subtle tears transformed into a full-on howl. Luckily for her, it just started to rain, so there was hardly anyone on the street outside or in the nearby park to hear. And the thunder with heavy raindrops was so loud, that even if there was someone, they still wouldn't hear her. She felt like she couldn't breathe. Everything in her chest was really tight. She stood up and walked back inside the room, when the pain hit again and made her whole body bend. It was really unbearable. She managed to sit on the floor before she collapsed, bent her knees, squeezed her stomach again and leaned her back against the bed. She felt like the pain was not going to stop. Her crying was hysterical, her breath quick and shallow. She curled up on the floor, hugging herself chest, and started to rethink the whole situation.

The truth was that she wasn't really angry with Bjørn or Matilde, she was angry with herself. Angry that she let herself put her guard down, trust someone again. Erica knew that all those tears weren't really about Wednesday Guy; it was just that this feeling had happened *yet* again. That she let it happen *yet* again. How many times would she fool herself that this time would be different, that this time it would work? She'd meet somebody who would actually want her. Because this breakdown wasn't really about Bjørn or even any guy, it was all about how low it made her. She was a smart woman, there must be a reason that she was the only person nobody, absolutely nobody wanted! It was as if she was cursed or something.

And there she was yet again. On the floor, lying in a familiar position, writhing like a worm in agony. She remembered every single word and compliment Bjørn had told her and that hurt the most. For a second, she felt like her world was collapsing and nothing would make it better. Nothing except time. That's all she needed. She just wanted to do what she usually did when it happened. Have a good long cry and wallow. She wanted to do a *Gilmore Girls,* like Lorelai advising her daughter to get back into her pyjamas and eat nothing but ice cream and pizza and cry. Then Erica's thoughts turned to her own mother, who died before she was born, who she never met but missed incredibly. She wondered if she would have been as supportive as Lorelai was to Rory in the TV show. She tried to calm herself down. Usually what would happen would be she'd have few more drinks, watch sad movie and go to bed, but this time was different. She wasn't at home now. She was just about to get up from the floor, her chest sore, her face red and puffy, when the phone rang. She glanced at it. It wasn't Bjørn. She wasn't really in a mood to talk to anybody, but it was Professor Wright, so she decided to answer the call.

'Hall,' her voice was rough, so she cleared her throat, 'ehm, hallo?'

'Dr Skyberg, it's Roger here.'

I know, I have caller ID. I know how technology works, I'm a Viking expert, not a Viking myself, you know! She looked for a tissue and said out loud, 'How can I help you, Professor?'

'I have managed to persuade Chairman Applegate to let you examine the compass.'

Ah, some good news! 'Really?' her voice became suddenly cheerful. 'Thank you Professor, I can't wait to put my hands on it tomorrow.'

'Actually, I don't know if this is a right moment.' He paused for a second. 'But I have it here in my house right now. I could send a car to bring you here, if that's not too late of course.'

Erica caught her puffy reflection in the mirror, but she was smiling. ‘There is no such thing as wrong moment or too late when it comes to Vikings. Please send the car,’ and she hang up.

Excitement took over. Erica couldn’t believe what she was about to do. She went to the bathroom to wash her face and re-apply makeup to cover up any signs of her meltdown.

Chapter 15

Although it was only a short distance in between the hotel's main entrance and the car, and then the car and door into Professor Wright's house, Erica managed to get soaking wet. So, when Roger opened the big wooden white door, she had only one thought and she decided to say it out loud:

'What is wrong with this weather? Every day, I swear, every single day, it is so incredibly hot – blue skies, sun shining – and then by night not just plain old raining, oh no, but a storm and literally it's pouring down with rain. Listen! I am guessing that we can expect thunder any second, now.' Roger was helping her to take off her wet coat, which had stuck to her body from the wet, and she was talking as they had known each other for ages and she was just visiting him casually. 'Seriously,' she went on, 'maybe this crazy weather does have something to do with the climate change and all those protesting activists up there are right!'

'Are you done, Doctor' said Roger with a smile and nodding his head, added, 'You are a very interesting character. Please, come on in. I'll make some tea.' He pointed to the sofa. For a split second he thought he was having déjà vu: wet guest, sitting on the same sofa, waiting for him while he made a pot of tea. But that was an old solicitor while this was… something else. He went and put the kettle on and came back to the living room.

'So? Can I see it?' she said with obvious excitement.

'Yes, of course' Roger answered. He came back from the kitchen to put the cup of tea in front of her. Then he walked over to the small wooden desk in the corner of the room, opened a drawer and took the compass that was hidden in a navy handkerchief. 'Just please, be careful with it,' he said and instantly regretted it. Her face reacted in a way to say: 'Seriously, you are telling *me* that?'

Erica took off her shoes and sat on the sofa in lotus style pose. She uncovered the compass and looked at it very closely for such a long time, that Roger finally said:

'Your tea will be cold soon.'

'Oh, yes, thank you, sorry. It's just. I have never seen anything like this before!' she said, touching the Vegvisir through the handkerchief. 'It looks like metal, but at the same time is very light. Vikings used the same material to make their coins, you know.' She raised her palm up and down several times, as she had to prove that it was not heavy indeed. She tried to guess its weight.

'Last time,' Roger began, 'at the museum, you mentioned that these are not Viking Runes?'

'Yes, you see, in Viking times they shortened the runic alphabet from 24 to 16 runes and just used some of them as two letters because they sounded very similar.'

'What do you mean?' Roger interrupted not really knowing what she meant.

'So,' Erica wondered how much she should explain to this curator, a historian himself. Then she remembered he'd asked her here for a reason and continued: 'Anglo-Saxons did something quite opposite – as you know their alphabet was longer. Vikings wanted to have as simple life as possible, so they decided that they didn't need all the letters from the original Old, or Elder if you wish to call it that, Futhark. The runic alphabet. It might be harder to notice it for you because in English some of the letters even from the modern European alphabet, are pronounced differently. So, like your "e" is my "i" etc.'

'Okay, I'm with you so far,' said Roger.

'For Vikings, letters like "b" and "p", "g" and "k" or "d" and "t" sound the same, so they decided to simplify it.' She turned the compass over in her hands. 'But I'm guessing there is a hidden meaning behind the fact that this compass is from the Viking Age but the runes around it – on that disc, see – are in Older Futhark.'

Roger strained to see the disc, then said: 'You keep saying Futhark, but you mean Futhorc, like the first six letters of the alphabet, correct?'

'I believe that is an Anglo-Saxon name, Professor, but yes, it is named after the first six runes: ***F**ehu,* ***U**ruz,* ***Th**urisaz,* ***A**nsuz,* ***R**aido* and ***K**aunan* – FUTHARK –' she said and reached for a tea. The coaster was a little further than she expected, so she lost her balance and a few drops of tea landed on the compass. Without hesitating, she used the handkerchief to quickly wipe them off, hoping that Roger hadn't seen, but then she put the mug down carefully and whispered, 'Holy Odin!'

'What? What happened? Did you spill tea on it?'

'Ah…'

'Did you damage it?' He quickly got up from the armchair he was sitting on and rushed over to Erica.

'No, but look, the disc! The disc… you can spin it around!' She was spinning the shield like it was a combination padlock. 'It looks like if you'll place it in the right spot and enter a code, it might open something up somewhere!'

Roger's eyes twinkled. 'I think I know where,' he said and disappeared for a second leaving Erica shouting with curiosity after him 'What do you mean!'

He came back few minutes later holding a small black tube.

'Do you remember, yesterday I mentioned a letter I received from my ancestor?' he asked, slowly taking an item out of the tube.

'Yes, yes! I got so occupied with the compass, that I nearly forgot! You mentioned before that it has some runic inscriptions you do not understand. The letter, can you show it to me?'

'The truth to be told, I lied a little bit. Well, maybe not lied but stretched some facts.'

'What do you mean?' asked Erica clearly confused and a little suspicious.

‘I mean, I did get a letter from my great-grandfather but that’s not the end. I also got this map with it,’ he said unfolding it in front of her. ‘Can you read any of *those* runic inscriptions, too?’

Erica took the map in her hands. It felt rough and smooth at the same time.

‘Animal skin. Deer’s?’ she said. She smelt it – what for Roger seemed a little bit disgusting and carried on: ‘It must be. The Vikings loved and admired stags. It was, because of Dáinn, Dvalinn, Duneyrr and Duraþrór, the four hearts believed to live in the World Tree of Yggdrasill. The Vikings could have admired squirrels, ravens, serpents, wolfs, but somehow the deer was the one. Maybe because it looks like reindeer?’ She was thinking out loud.

Roger took a sip of his tea and said with friendly laugh, ‘Doctor, can we please get back to the map?’ and at the same time it went through his head, *She really has no clue how passionate she can talk about this subject and how really easily she adds much irrelevant information, too. But I think it’s cute.* She interrupted him with:

‘What is it though? A map of some town tattooed in black ink? But then, what are those coloured lines?’

‘Dr Skyberg, I’ll explain that in a minute. But the inscriptions?’

‘Oh yes, yes, apologies, it’s just so fascinating!’ She smelled the animal’s skin again and said ‘Okay, I can see one at the very top, like it could be a title or name and four runic inscriptions, positioned on twelve, three, six and nine o’clock. The letters are not clear though. Look – can I have a pen and something to write on?’ she asked without taking her eyes from the map. Her mouth was slightly open, eyes blinking. When Roger brought her what she asked for, she transferred the runic letters onto the piece of paper:

Her lips were moving, but not even a sound came out of them. She counted using her fingers and nodding her head. Roger stood up from his armchair and sat next to Erica on the sofa. What he understood from her actions was that she was just guessing each individual rune and translating, one by one into the modern alphabet. But when he sat closer to her he realised, that she was in fact *saying* something. She was very quietly murmuring the whole alphabet back and forth and when she got to a certain letter, she wrote it below the appropriate rune.

'Gebo, Wunjo, Hagalaz,' her hand counted seven, eight, nine. She had just written some letters underneath the runes she managed to recognise, when outside a powerful clap of thunder reverberated above them.

And the power in Roger's house went off.

Curiously, they both reacted in exactly the same way: no panic, just complete silence. They both seemed to be waiting for something to happen next. After a few seconds that felt more like minutes, Roger stood up. Erica heard him swear something about his phone being off, and also heard him trip over a couple of times and hit against objects clearly standing in his way. Eventually he came back with two big, blazing candles in his hands.

'Scented candles?' Erica said with surprise. She sniffed. 'Jasmine?' This was the last thing she expected him to possess but took one of them in her free hands.

'What?' He felt caught out as he knew that she already guessed they were to impress women on a date. 'Yes, I am a guy and I have nice scented Yankee Candles in my house. I like to create a romantic atmosphere from time to time when I have lady guests over. So, sue me,' he answered with a little laugh in his voice. 'My phone is nearly dead and all my torches are in a cupboard somewhere, and as you probably just heard, me walking around the house in complete darkness it is not something safe.'

The rain outside was pounding heavier and heavier, the thunder louder and louder.

'I'm saying nothing,' said Erica. She looked back at the map, feeling that the professor was watching her. Suddenly, she cleared her throat and yelled:

'Holy Odin!'

'You really like this saying, huh?' Roger commented, his voice cheerful.

'Holy Odin, holy Odin, holy Odin, look!' she shouted again, completely ignoring his comment. 'Look at this!'

As soon as Roger brought his candle a little closer to the map, he realised what was she talking about. Under the light from the candle's flame all of a sudden, in the top right corner, additional inscription appeared. Two rows with six individual squares, some of them with rune inside.

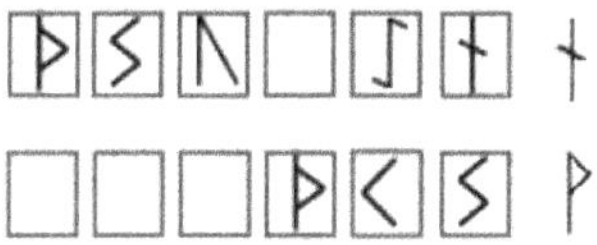

Erica was so excited. 'Okay, if you can take the map and hold your light closer to this bit here, Professor, so I can write it down.' She pointed to the top of the map, put her candle down on the table and grabbed the pen and paper again. 'Wait, that's too close now, can you hold the map a little bit further?' she said and gently pushed away his hand.

'Erica!' Roger shouted calling her by her name for the first time. 'Look what you're doing!'

'Helvete!' she yelled. She'd pulled his hand away a little too forcefully, so that the map touched the candle and a few sparks caught where there were a few short deer hairs.

'Shit. I am so sorry!' Erica watched in panic, Roger gently putting the fire out with a blanket from the sofa. 'Please, forgive me, I'll be more careful, I promise–'

‘–Or maybe you shouldn’t be.’ Roger’s voice was excited. He stood up from where he was kneeling on the floor and showed her back of the map.

‘What is it?’ Erica said. ‘It looks like there’s some symbol hidden there.’

‘Yes, I think so too. Let me find my lighter.’ He reached into the front pocket of his jeans and put the map back on the glass table. They both kneeled, looked at each other, took a deep breath and watched. Parts of the deer hair disappeared only to create a great symbol right in the centre. Erica stared at it. She knew she’d seen it before, but where…

‘That’s impossible,’ she said.

‘What is impossible?’ asked Roger in curious voice.

‘The symbol, the symbol right here.’ She pointed at the centre of the slightly burnt skin. ‘I have seen it before at least once in my life. I have definitely seen it.’

‘Where?’

Erica looked at him and shrugged. Roger rubbed his eyes.

‘Erica, I mean Doctor Skyberg, when and where have you seen this symbol? This could be crucial information! I believe from what my great-grandfather told me through that letter, that he although didn’t find Einarr’s tomb, he found the grave of a Viking who was trying to find Einarr’s tomb. To follow the treasure. That’s why he had a map and the compass.’ His voice started to rise. ‘Maybe this symbol can tell us something more! So please, think!’ he said in a begging tone.

‘I am trying! Trust me, Professor, it’s not that easy. I have seen many symbols in my life and some of them are very similar to each other.’ She sat down on the sofa. ‘So please let me think for a second–’

Then someone knocked on the front door.

‘Who’s that?’ Erica asked with slight panic in her voice and quickly put her shoes back on. ‘Are you expecting someone?’

Roger blew out the candles hoping that whoever it was would think there was nobody home and leave. Sadly, it caused a completely different reaction. A second later, they heard a great cracking sound, like a gunshot used to break the lock. Erica snatched up the map and compass and felt Roger grab her hand. They stood in the middle of his living room, not speaking, holding hands, waiting for the worst to happen.

Chapter 16

A hooded figure stood right outside Roger's house. He pointed his gun in front of him and fired. He blew the lock off. Carefully he pushed the white wooden door open and walked inside. He turned on the little torch which was hanging on the string around his wrist and looked around. He wasn't stupid. He'd seen from the outside the gentle candlelight in the living room and now just a small trail of smoke above the coffee table. He approached and gently touched both candle jars. They were still incredibly hot. He looked around again. There was nobody. *Where did they go?* he thought. *Definitely not upstairs, I would have seen them. So, either they are still hiding here, or they used the back door and left through the garden.* A cold breeze coming from the back room indicated that some door or window was open. He was just about to leave the room, when something on the sofa caught his eye. *Interesting.* He looked at the piece of paper with runic inscriptions, took out his phone and quickly pressed Number 1 on speed dial.

'It's me,' said his softly pitched voice. 'You were right, they've discovered something.'

'Have you seen it? Do you know what it is?'

'No, they managed to escape. But I've found something interesting, I'm just sending you a picture.' He waited a moment then said, 'Did you get it?'

'Yes, I'm looking at it right now,' said voice on the other side of the phone. 'Good job. Now go and try to find them. They might already know where the real ring is. I will deal with this inscription and keep you posted. And you, of course, will do the same.'

'Of course.' The hooded figure hung up, and slowly moved towards back door. It was indeed slightly open. He stepped out back and looked around. The thunder and rain had stopped and there was absolutely nobody within sight.

He watched as the power flicked back on to a couple of neighbouring houses, drawing closer to him.

I'd better go, he thought, *before someone notices me.*

Chapter 17

Erica ran. Even though she had these amazingly long legs, she hated any sports and especially activities like running. But she ran as fast as she could. Her life could depend on it.

It was that weird hour when very late night and very early morning were meeting together, so although it was getting brighter outside, still far away the sun had yet to show his face to this side of the world. The rain stopped, as they ran, but the cold was still palpable in the air. Erica felt it on her face, on her skin. They had left Roger's house in such a rush, that neither of them had a chance to grab a coat.

After what it seemed to her like a marathon or at least half marathon, Roger finally stopped. They were both breathing loudly. Roger, hands on thighs trying to regulate his heartbeat; Erica, squeezing the stitch in her left side.

'What… the… hell… just–' she had to take a few quick breaths in and out as she struggled to finish the sentence '–happened.'

'Are you okay, Doctor?'

'I think, after tonight's events, Professor, it would be alright if we started to call each other by our names,' she wheezed. Despite the situation she smiled and put her hand out.

'Very well,' he panted. He shook her hand and smiled back.

'So where are we, what's the plan?' asked Erica, straightening up.

Roger looked around. They were alone in the middle of a park. They could only hear but not see the drunk people coming back home from the clubs. Roger squinted. The familiar sight of mist rising over the lake, made him say 'We're in St. James's Park, not too far from my house...'

‘That doesn’t tell me anything, I still don’t know where we are. Is my hotel far from here?’

‘Quite. I mean, still manageable, but I am not sure if that is the safe place now either.’

‘What?’ Erica started to panic. She was cold. ‘What now? What now, what now, what now?’

‘Are you alright–?’

‘Let’s get the facts straight. We can’t go back to your house; we can’t go to my hotel. Your phone is dead, someone just tried to kill us, and we have absolutely no clue what to do next.’

Roger nodded. ‘That is exactly right. It’s too late for any pub to be still open, yet too early for any café to be already open. How bizarre is that?’ He stared at her. ‘Wait, don’t you have your phone on you?’ Roger asked with hope in his voice.

She reached to the pocket and looked at the black screen. She hadn’t charged it since the FaceTime earlier. ‘Helvete, dead as well. What is this technology good for, if you can’t use it when you need it!’

‘Let’s just keep it cool, there must be solution and I bet it’s closer than we think.’

‘Phone box!’ Erica screamed with excitement and pointed to the street. ‘God bless your old school red telephone boxes! Can you call someone?’

‘Hmmm let me think. I do have some change in my pocket but who can I call at this time, let’s face it.’

‘Uh, I know! Call your PA, Tony. I am sure, he will be more than happy to help.’

‘Yes, but I don’t remember his number by heart. I’ve never had to!’

‘Wait a minute,’ she reached to the back pocket of her jeans. ‘Oddly, I have his card. He gave it to me when he gave me a ride from the airport, you know, just in case.’

Roger smiled and started marching towards the booth. He stepped inside and nearly passed out. ‘I guess for some people it is a modern-day toilet, not an old times communication system.’ He pinched his nose and tried again. He dialled the number from the card. After a few rings, the sleepy voice of his PA answered:

'Hello?'

'Tony?'

'Nnnhmmm?'

'Professor Wright here. Listen, I know it's late, but I have a huge favour to ask. I think myself and Doctor Skyberg might be in danger. Could we possibly stay at your place tonight? I wouldn't ask if it wasn't important.'

The voice on the other end of the phone woke up. 'Of course, absolutely, Professor. I'll text you the address,' said Tony who was just about to hang up, when Roger stopped him.

'No, wait! I'm calling from the phone booth; my phone is dead. Tell me your address, I'll write it down.' He signalled to Erica to pass him a pen.

'I'm down in Brixton. Just get the Night Tube and I'll meet you at the station.' Tony gave the instruction and hung up.

'Brixton,' said Roger to Erica.

'Is that far?'

'Tube from Green Park.'

'Is that far?' Erica repeated.

'No,' Roger assured her, 'Green Park station is very close. Are you alright to walk?'

Erica looked at her wet shoes and nodded silently.

'We will have a minute or two to rest and hopefully it'll be warmer than outside,' Roger said. Ten minutes later, they were sitting on the platform at Green Park, waiting for the Victoria line train to come.

The carriage was nearly empty, apart from a man who fell asleep on the priority seat, leaning against glass barrier. *So, this is how people party in London* went through Erica's mind. She and Roger sat in silence, both following closely on the Tube map above their heads every single stop. Eventually one of them decided to speak.

‘Right,’ Roger broke off the silence, ‘I think we should talk about our map, before we arrive at Tony’s.’ His voice was low and secretive. ‘And we need a story to tell him. Don’t get me wrong, I trust him, but I don’t think it’s the right moment to tell him everything.’

‘Everything what? The two of us don’t know that much just yet,’ Erica said. She grabbed an abandoned *Evening Standard* newspaper from the neighbouring seat, spread it out next to her, took out the piece of rolled skin from the little black tube, which she’d grabbed before they ran, and discreetly unfolded their mystery map. *Good thinking,* thought Roger. *She’s resourceful, isn’t she*?

Erica peered at the map. ‘Hmmmm, where were we? Hidden inscription, yes.’ She touched its surface very gently. ‘I assume we cannot use the lighter in here, but at least I can try to make sense of the stuff I have managed to write down at your house.’

Roger stared at her, waiting for her to begin but instead, she held out her hand, staring back at him and not even trying to check her belt bag or pockets.

‘Roger? The piece of paper, thanks?’ She stretched her hand out further. ‘Now, would be a good time to give it to me.’

‘Wait, what? You think I have it? I thought you had it!’

‘No, I have only two hands. I grabbed the compass and the map!’

‘I guess it must be still in my house. What if the intruder found it?’

‘Okay let’s think. Don’t panic, don’t panic.’ She was more trying to calm herself than him. ‘It didn’t make sense anyway. As far as I remember the first line said *thsuynn* or something like that, which make no sense at all. So, if you never told anyone about the letter and the map, they might think that it was something you were working on for fun.’

‘Could be. Possible…’ He was looking somewhere far in space. ‘Apart that, this person wanted something from my house, which was clearly worth even killing for.’

‘Okay, let’s just look at the map and see what we can make of it now. We assume that the town on it is London. That is the River Thames, but still, London’s so big, it’s going to be hard to narrow it down.’

‘Is there anything that indicates where to start? Any special symbol, anything? We must start somewhere.’ Roger was thinking out loud.

‘Ladies and gentlemen, this is your driver. We are approaching our last stop, change, all change. Please mind the gap and don’t forget to take your belongings with you. Thank you for travelling with London Underground.’

Erica quickly rolled the map back into the black tube and they left the train. They followed the endless ‘way out’ signs, walked through long corridors and used a few escalators to get back up to the surface. All of a sudden it hit Roger: ‘I know where to start! We should–’

‘Tony!’ Erica interrupted before Roger managed to finish the thought. ‘It’s so great to see you again.’

‘Hello Dr Skyberg’ he shook her hand and then nodded at Roger ‘Professor.’

‘We really are grateful, Tony. You know I wouldn’t call you if I didn’t have any other option,’ said Roger.

‘Yes, but you were very mysterious over the phone, I believe I deserve some explanation.’

‘Of course you do. Apologies. Tony, this is strictly between the three of us. Until we’ll find out more, we cannot trust anybody.’ When he noticed his PA’s expression, he hurried up with an explanation. ‘Somebody broke into my house. We don’t know why, if he or she were acting alone, or if they were looking for something, but we can’t ignore the fact that they used a gun to destroy the lock. I think might be connected to the robbery at the museum and… this person wouldn’t hesitate to use it against human being either.’

‘What?’ Tony was clearly shocked. ‘Are you hurt?’

‘No, no,’ said Erica. ‘We are both fine, we just had to run, that’s why we didn’t have any place to go.’

‘I’m glad you called me then,’ he smiled. Erica noticed again what a nice smile he had.

‘Tony, listen, I know that this is not listed at your job description,’ Roger stepped in. ‘So I want you to know that I really appreciate it.’

‘No problem, Professor. Anytime.’

Chapter 18

Erica and Roger followed Tony through the streets of South London. For Erica, it looked like they had travelled to some place completely different. The houses, people, *everything* was different to what she had seen so far since her arrival in England's capital city. She thought it was funny though that, although she was far from home, with completely no sense of her whereabouts, trying to hide from a potentially dangerous person, with two men she barely knew, she felt completely safe. She also was glad deep inside, that all this happened tonight, so she had no time to rethink the Bjørn–Matilde situation.

Tony's place was definitely the last thing Erica or even Roger expected. Naturally, they thought it was going to be a shared flat or house, but instead it was a warehouse converted to a living space.

'Come on in.' Tony encouraged them to come inside. 'Everyone is asleep or still at work, so don't worry.' He led them further in. On the way to the main part of the living space, he grabbed a black hoodie from the hook by the main door and passed it to slightly shaking Erica. 'Here, madam, this should warm you up. I can put the kettle on as well, unless you would like to get some sleep.' He looked at her waiting for an answer.

'I think sleep for now sounds good,' said Roger. 'We need to have clear, rested minds in order to think straight and plan what to do next.' He looked at the clock above the TV. It was half past four in the morning.

'Right,' said Tony. 'Bathroom is at the end just over there, another toilet right by the main door. Lucky for you, someone just moved out two days ago, so we have one spare room, but unless you want to sleep together, the other person will have to take this sofa,' he pointed down.

'I'll take the sofa,' said Roger very quickly in a tone that nobody even dared to argue with him.

Erica followed Tony up the metal stairs and quickly turned around. Roger was getting comfortable on the sofa in the living room, which she noticed was connected to the dining area and the kitchen, open plan. The room she was about to spend the night in was almost empty, as expected for one recently vacated, but there was at least comfortable looking made up bed. Tony brought her an extra blanket, which she accepted, as well as reassured she was so tired, that cold won't keep her awake. After all, she was coming from Norway.

'Do you need anything else?' he asked before leaving the room.

'It would be nice to charge my phone,' she said hopefully. When Tony arrived with his spare charger, she wished him sweet dreams and finally getting the hint, he left her alone.

Erica lay down on what she wrongly judged at first to be a very comfortable mattress. She closed her eyes and waited for the moment when she would finally fall asleep. Unfortunately, even though the body was exhausted, her brain decided that it was better to go over recent events right at this very moment and was not allowing her to drift away.

She changed sides, changed again, lay on her back, on her belly. Nothing seemed to be helping. She finally gave up, stopped fighting it and let her brain think about whatever it wanted to. Of course, there was Bjørn. And Matilde. There was a matter of why Erica had such a crappy love-life again and if she would ever live happily after. Then she thought about the discovery at Roger's: the spinning disc around the Vegvisir, with its Runes, the map with mysterious inscriptions and that symbol at the back. *The symbol. I know I have seen it before. I just know it* – she was trying so hard to remember where and when, that she hadn't noticed, she'd finally given up and fell asleep.

Shortly afterwards, Erica suddenly woke up. She sat straight up on the bed, her heart thumping fast. At first, she had absolutely no clue where she was. She still felt very tired. She looked around curious what time it was, but unfortunately for her there was no clock in the room. Then she remembered that Tony brought her a charger earlier that night, so her phone was probably ready to get back to life again. She picked it up from the floor, turned it on, entered the password and stopped herself – she realised that she was kind of hoping that she would find a message from the Wednesday Guy or Matilde, or both of them. It would say that this was a big mistake and misunderstanding or it would at least be apologising for doing that to her.

Nothing.

She looked at the time. It was nearly seven o'clock in the morning. Behind the window, the sun was slowly coming up. Complete silence prevailed and indicated that the rest of the place was still asleep. She placed her hand on her chest. Her heart was racing. *What is going on? What happened? Have I just had a nightmare?* She tried to remind herself what she had been dreaming about. She glanced at her phone again. For some reason, she carefully checked the time and the date again. *Mum!* she gasped and all of a sudden felt fully awake. *For the first time in thirty years, I will not be able to visit your grave at the anniversary of your death! How could I forget!* She felt a little sick. *Maybe I can ask Granny to put flowers down for me. I am sure she will be going to the cemetery. If it's today, that also means it's... my birthday.* Erica Skyberg never celebrated her birthday. Never in her life. For her it was the day when her mother died. There was nothing cheerful in it, nothing to be thankful for. Her head was a mess. Around a thousand thoughts buzzed at the same time, but there was one which clearly stood out. *Cemetery? Wait a minute, Oh Holy Odin!* She shot up from the bed as if it was on fire and she had to escape from flames. *The symbol! The symbol on the back of the map.* She started to walk from wall to wall, back and forth. *That's impossible! Could it... could it be exactly the same as the one on my mother's gravestone?*

Chapter 19

Roger didn't want to be awake just yet, but the noise coming from the kitchen wouldn't let him sleep. He tried to ignore it, covered his ears with the pillow, put the duvet over his head. Whoever was in the kitchen clearly wasn't really bothered they were disturbing someone. A few minutes later Roger heard the sound of a plate being put on the long wooden table in the dining area. The TV opposite the sofa he was sleeping on came to life. He sat up and looked behind him. A tall, skinny but with quite muscly arms brunette was eating a cereal. She looked at him with a mouth full of muesli and started to choke. Roger without hesitation got up and ran to her. He was just about to do the Heimlich manoeuvre, when the girl started to cough and just showed him with the hand gesture, to pat her on the back. He noticed a tattoo on girl's forearm. *Very similar to the one Tony has,* he thought.

'Are you okay?' Professor asked with concern.

'Yeah, I'm fine, thanks,' she smiled and without any questions got back to her breakfast.

'Oh, apologies. I'm Roger, I am Tony's–'

'Friend from work,' a familiar voice finished the sentence.

Roger didn't know why his PA just lied but decided to go with it and didn't object.

'Morning guys, coffee anyone?' Tony came down the stairs.

'Tea, if I may,' replied Roger. 'You can make one coffee as well, I'll take it to Erica.' He added and began to wonder why the girl sat at the table wasn't questioning his presence.

'This is Annabel, by the way, my sister,' Tony pointed at the girl, 'and she wasn't really choking. She just likes to freak people out, as she thinks it's funny.'

‘Oh, good one,’ Roger nodded with sarcasm. ‘So you guys are used to having visitors?’

‘It would be strange if we didn’t’ started Annabel, but Tony finished for her. ‘Seven people live here, we all have friends, other halves and so on. Yes, we’re used to having visitors.’

At this moment another person walked in, took the remote from the dining table, said good morning, turned up the telly and sat on one of the sofas.

‘Hey, Tony! There is something about this stolen ring you were so interested in the other day.’

Within seconds all of them stood right in front of TV carefully listening what Detective O’Sullivan has to say.

‘We are still investigating circumstances, and we are still looking for the ring. But Mike’s family deserves to say goodbye to him. All the evidence is secured, and his funeral will take place today in the afternoon. Please, act with respect.’ Charlie ignored questions from the reporters and simply walked away.

Shit, my phone. There must be thousands of messages from the detective and Chairman Applegate! Roger thought and turned to his PA. ‘Tony, do you have a phone charger I can borrow? I forgot to ask last night.’

‘I have a spare one, but I gave it to Doctor Skyberg.’ He realised that his flatmates were looking at him confused and were just about to tease him for his work-talk, so he added, ‘I mean Erica. I gave it to Erica before she went to bed. Do you want me to get it for you?’

‘Oh no, it’s fine, let her sleep. I’ll grab it, when she leaves the room,’ said Roger, looking upstairs.

***

Luckily for Erica, the room she was staying in was right at the end of the hall. There was only a very small chance that somebody would hear if she was awake or not. She wanted to leave the room but didn’t want to face questions. And at this moment, what she needed were answers.

I knew I'd seen that symbol before, but what if I'm wrong? What if I am jumping to conclusions and the symbols are just very similar? There is so many signs which look pretty much the same... No. I cannot do that to myself right know. I cannot doubt my gut and my judgement. I can just ask Sofie. It makes no sense but there's no harm in looking for answers. Anyway, she wouldn't lie to me. I am sure, there is an explanation. Yes. There must be.

After convincing herself that there was no other option, Erica picked up the phone and shortly after heard a lovely, familiar voice saying hello on the other side of the line.

'Hi, Sofie, I am so sorry to bother you, especially at this time. You must be crazy busy serving breakfast, but it's kind of important. Do you have a second?'

'No, no, don't apologise, my dear. Your uncle Olaf is helping me. He knows what day it is today and that I am not always in top shape then.'

'It won't take long, but it's about my mother. Do you remember you once told me that Mum was interested in the symbols old Norwegian families would have, like a coat of arms, that sort of thing?'

'Yes,' said Sofie.

'Did she ever mention that our family might have one?'

'Why, yes. I always thought it was her rich imagination and desire to discover something mysterious in life, but then after she died, I noticed that the very similar symbol she once described to me, appeared on her gravestone.'

'You never told me that. Why?'

'Oh honey, you were pretty much just born then and later I figured that if it was the truth your grandmother would tell you,' said Sofie in a gentle and apologetic voice.

'So, you think that Gran Greta knows?' Erica couldn't believe in that. She and Granny didn't have secrets. Neither big nor small. None.

'I'm sure, yes. You might want to call and ask her. Sorry, I can't be more help. I have to go now but stay safe and honey—'

'—yes...?' Erica hoped she would say more about the symbol, but Sofie just added,

'Happy birthday.'

***

'Professor Wright, with all due respect, it is already noon. If we want to make it to Mike's funeral on time, we should get going,' Tony said. Roger stood right next to the metal stairs, waiting for Erica to leave her room.

'What if something's happened? We are going to leave without checking on her?'

'What could possibly happen?' said Tony. 'You said it yourself, you both had an eventful night. She's probably asleep. Besides, she never knew Mike anyway. Let's go, otherwise we'll be late. You still need to change. We can drop by your house. I will tell Benji,' he pointed at the half-asleep Indian guy on the couch, 'to text me when she is awake. He can tell her where we are.'

***

Erica woke up again. This time the sun was high in the sky. *It must be around noon*, she thought. *How long have I been asleep? And why does my head hurt so much? I remember, I was just about to do something but then... I passed out? What was I doing*? She sat up and rubbed her eyes. *Ah, I was about to call...*

'Hi Granny, it's me,' said Erica. At first, she pretended that everything was alright.

'Hello, my little one, are you okay? I can't believe that for the first time you are not here today!'

'I know. I know. Listen, there is something I need to talk to you about.'

'Absolutely, anything. Did something happen? Did the boy hurt you?' asked Greta with concern in her voice. It was as if she knew he would like as they always did. 'Or is it about your mum?'

'Actually, a little bit of everything. Can you tell me something more about the symbol on mum's gravestone? You know, the one in the left top corner?'

'Symbol? Oh, I don't know honey, it was perhaps something that came with the design? I never really noticed it at all, I…'

'Hadn't noticed it?'

'No, sweetheart. I'm going to the cem–'

'Sofie said it was a symbol of the Skyberg family. Sort of like a crest.'

'Sofie said?' Granny's voice sounded a little harder than before.

'So, is she right?' asked Erica.

'I really haven't noticed it…'

For a usually calm person, Erica was suddenly furious. Her grandmother was hiding something, and she didn't know why. She knew that it simply could not be a coincidence, that the symbol which Sofie said was a symbol of the Skyberg's family, would accidentally be on her mother's gravestone *as well as* on the map leading to Einarr's tomb. There had to be connection between the saga and Erica's family. She didn't know what kind of, but there certainly was one. And Granny must have known it.

Erica wasn't feeling herself. Her body was shaking, and she was slowly losing her patience.

'Gran, I know you are hiding something. I just know it. So, tell me, what is it? What are you not telling me?'

'Erica, this isn't really a phone conversation. Come back home, I'll explain everything.'

'No! You will tell me everything right here, right now. That symbol. I've just seen it on a map leading to Einarr's tomb and the treasure. So, what does our family have to do with the saga and all this mess?'

'You have it? You saw it?' Greta couldn't contain her excitement.

'Oh, so I am right?' all the sudden Erica's voice softened. 'Gran, tell me, please.' She took a deep breath and braced herself to whatever would happen next.

Granny Greta Skyberg clicked her teeth, then spoke clearly, gently and slowly. 'First, you must know, that this was never the way how you were supposed to find out. And before you ask, yes, you were about to find out. Maybe not now, but one day for sure.'

Habit took over. Erica felt like she was about to hear a bedtime story from her gran, like when she was little. She sat down on the bed, supported her back with the pillow, stretched her legs, and listened to her gran's voice…

It happened when I was probably around three, maybe four years old. My mum was putting me down to bed, even though it was earlier than usual. She had somewhere important to be, so decided to tell me a quick story to make me sleep. That story, from then on, she was telling me pretty much every single night. It was about a magnificent Viking hero named Einarr. About his love for Princess Ingrid and betrayal by both she and Einarr's brother Audun. It was a story about love and a curse. About choosing to be lonely forever.

Greta Skyberg paused in the telling then carried on with the story.

But only when I was a little bit older, did I discover something quite strange. Everybody in all of Norway seemed to know the saga, and in every single telling, in every source it ended exactly the same: Einarr lost his life during the battle with Anglo-Saxons in England, an awful plague killed Ingrid, and Audun committed suicide.

But for some reason I knew more.

I knew for example, that Einarr had mistakenly given the cursed ring to Audun. And that, after he killed himself, Hertha found and took the ring back.

I knew this because my mother told it to me. But what right did I have to question if what my mother told me was or wasn't true? Maybe she just wanted to colour the story, add a few more details here and there. And in the end, who was she to know these tiny but how very important details?

One night, after she'd told me the story yet again, and thought I was asleep, she left. But I wasn't asleep. I followed her. I followed her through the nearby woods, to the forest clearing. I hid in the bushes and witnessed something I have never, ever seen before in my life. The night was pitch black; the sky full of stars. Every now and then I heard a wolf not far away from us howling to the moon. In the clearing were people. It was like secret assembly, which could have been mistaken for a witches' sabbath. Even I thought it was. Around the fire, just over a dozen characters in long fur cloaks with hoods were watching the single person in the middle of the circle. This woman was holding a huge hand carved walking stick, waving with it and shouting something in Old Norwegian. From the fire, sparks began to float in the air, one by one forming themselves into runes. The rest happened even quicker. The people in cloaks started move clockwise around the blaze muttering something like a spell or incantation, as they watched the runes soaring up into the sky. The person in the middle of the circle all of a sudden fell into a trance.

And poof! *like that, disappeared.*

Where she just stood, a black raven appeared and flew away.

Scared someone would discover me, I ran home. I couldn't sleep that night. I kept waiting to hear the front door go, but my mum never came back. The next day, I told everything to my dad. He was angry. I have never seen him in such state. He started to yell at me: 'Your mother! Your mother! She just had to follow the steps of that damned Hertha! This is all her fault. Damned Völva. Your mum promised me she would stop!' It was like he was ranting. 'I knew that her heritage would eventually get her one day. But not you! No. I promise I will protect you, my child.' Within a few hours we had packed out things, left the house and never came back. All I took of Mums was a ring – I didn't know what it was then – and a few clothes. Dad never mentioned any of it again and I never asked. But I did my own research. Hertha was a Völva – a Reader of the Runes. She could get herself into the magic trance of Seidr during which their spirit leaving the body could transform into an animal. But that is not what I witnessed.

Greta stopped for few seconds to catch a deeper breath. Erica could have sworn she hear tears running down her granny's cheek, but she didn't say anything. She patiently waited for her to continue…

Years later, I was briefly happy again. I had a wonderful husband and a beautiful daughter. Unfortunately, my husband died during the war, and it was just the two of us, your mum and me. She was a baby. I didn't have anyone beside her. She was my everything. But then your infelicitous father came along. I tried many things to separate the two of them, but nothing seemed to be working. They kept saying that they found true love. True love! Impossible.

And then, just in time to hear that your mother is pregnant, I reminded myself about the ring I took with me. Einarr's cursed ring. So, I tricked your father in taking that ring and to propose to my baby. It worked. Not long before you were born, he disappeared, and for a short while it was just the two of us again. My darling Julie and me.

And then, too quickly, another dark day came along. I wasn't enough for my daughter. She was so very lonely. All she would be talking about was you. How badly she couldn't wait to see you, how she doesn't need anyone else. It hurt. I did everything to have her back, but I still felt invisible.

At the hospital, it didn't go well. When they told me that she had died giving birth to you Erica, I wanted to punish you. I hated you in that moment. In my eyes, you were responsible for all of that. For taking her. Even though I wasn't cursed, it felt like I was. And I wanted you to feel exactly the same. So, when you were a child, I gave you the very same ring your father used to propose to your mother. Because it belonged to her, you never questioned it. Years went by and my anger was gone. But it was too late. The legend stands, that it's enough to wear the ring for nine hours and to be cursed forever. I'm sorry.'

Even though neither of them said anything, they could hear each other's breath.

'Erica? Erica, are you still there?'

'Stop. Shush. Don't say anything.'

'But Erica, it was years ago, I didn't—'

'Not even one more word. I can't listen to this now.' She hung up, lay down and passed out again.

Chapter 20

Erica sat on the bed holding her head in between her legs, as if she were going to be sick. She felt like the whole world was spinning. Someone knocked on the door. She didn't answer. After a while the person knocked once again and slowly opened the door.

'Erica? Are you…' Roger quickly came over to her, put the coffee he was holding down on the floor and grabbed her face into his hands 'I wanted to say, *awake*, but actually are you *okay*?' No reaction at all. She was kind of looking at him, but at the same time her sight seemed gone. Her face was red, covered in tears. She wasn't saying anything.

'Erica? Is everything alright?' Worried, he started to gently shake her body.

She looked at him, surprised by his presence. Out of the blue, her voice a little slurred, she asked, 'Do you think I'm pretty? Would you, Professor Roger Wright, find me attractive?'

Roger was taken aback and a little bit confused, but he could see in her face she was really serious. He quickly answered, 'Yes, of course. Of course! If not for the fact that we are working on the professional level—'

He hadn't even finished the sentence, when she tried to stand up but failed. She slumped down and interjected in a slightly mocking voice, 'Surely.'

'Surely what?'

'Surely something has to get in the way. The same as Bjørn wanted me, but Matilde came around, the same as my dad loved my mum but he still left her, the same as every guy…' She looked up at Roger. 'Oh my god, it actually makes sense!'

It made no sense to Roger. 'Erica, calm down, what are you talking about? What happened while I was gone? Did you have a bad dream?' And then, not sure what else to say he took the role of best friend: ‘You will find the right man, you’ll see. You just have to wait for the right moment, you—’

‘No, Roger, I won’t. And do you want to know why?’

‘Erm…’

‘That’s a rhetorical question so don’t answer. It’s because I’m cursed.’

‘Cursed?’

‘Yes. I am FREAKING CURSED!’ She started to sort of laugh and snort.

Roger picked up the coffee and offered it to her. She stared at it.

‘Erica, come downstairs, please,’ he said. ‘You haven’t eaten anything today. Once you have some food, you’ll feel better, trust me.’ He stretched his hand in the hope she would take it.

She suddenly noticed something about him. ‘Why are you so dressed up?’

‘Tony and I, we just got back from Mike’s funeral. It was a nice ceremony.’

‘Oh. You look nice. Smart.’

Roger nodded uncomfortably and said: ‘We ran into that detective – O’Sullivan – apparently, they have a break in the case. He mentioned something that he needs to talk to you about. He can meet us at the museum later today.’

She was just about to say something, when someone knocked on the door. It was the professor’s PA.

‘Hi Dr Skyberg, Professor, sorry to interrupt, but I thought the doctor might want to take a shower and change her clothes. Here,’ he passed to her a pile of towels, a fresh outfit and a few toiletries. ‘It’s my sister’s. Annabel went out, but I’m sure she won’t mind,’ he added, quickly noticing it might look strange.

‘Thank you, Tony, that’s very thoughtful,’ she took the stuff from his hands and, feeling a little better, stood up. ‘Roger, we will finish this conversation downstairs.’ And she left the room.

‘Oh, okay,’ said Roger to the thin air.

Roger, Tony and Benji sat on the sofa in front of TV, watching a programme on how climate change in the far north was affecting life over there and how very dangerous it was to the rest of the world, when Erica finally came downstairs. She looked different. And it wasn't only because Annabel's style was completely different to hers, but there was something else. She looked calm and determined. Roger stood up and came over to the dining table.

'Here, we ordered pizza,' he encouraged her to take slice from the box he held out. She grabbed a slice without saying anything but nodded a thanks and looked first at the TV, then at the sofa.

'Who's that?' she nodded at Benji, who'd already fallen asleep.

'That,' said Roger, 'is a very interesting resident of this warehouse.' Seeing her reaction to the word 'interesting', he quickly explained, 'I-I think he's stoned.'

'He is, he is. But he is also a good fella.' Tony came over and grabbed a slice of pizza as well. 'Right, if you don't mind, I have to go out to run a few errands. If you need me, call my mobile.'

Tony left. Besides the two of them and the now fully asleep Benji, there was no one else. They decided to use that moment to discuss the map.

'Erm,' Roger began. 'Are you—'

'Didn't you mention something that you know where to start looking for the tomb?' Erica whispered, cutting him off.

'Look, Erica, with all due respect, are you sure you are okay? Are you sure you want to continue this? You didn't look well earlier.'

'I am not crazy. Look, I spoke to my gran. And it was a bit of a shock. The symbol at the back of the map belongs to my family. Hertha, the Völva from the saga was my ancestor. The stolen ring from the British Museum was really, really a fake. I know this as I have the real one. In short, I am cursed.'

'Cursed?'

'Cursed, yes, keep up. And apparently when I was a baby, my grandmother, who I love and has always been there for me, hated me.'

'Erica…?'

'But that's okay now.' Her voice was getting high-pitched and strained. She brought it back down. 'Anyway, I have this feeling that the only way to break the curse is to find Einarr. He will be in possession of the other ring, I'm sure of it. Maybe if they are brought together the curse can be lifted?' She put both of her hands on her forehead and closed her eyes for a second. 'To be honest, I don't know. But I do *not* intend to stay cursed and lonely for the rest of my life, that is what I know for sure. I think thirty-two years is enough. And if there is even the slightest chance I can change it, believe me, Professor, I will.'

Roger looked at her in all seriousness. 'How do you know that everything your gran told you is true?'

'Look at this,' she put her hand on the kitchen table, 'I got this ring from my gran years ago. I was a child – I mean who curses a child! – but as the curse states I have always been lonely and every single time I meet a guy it doesn't work between us and it's something that I can't really explain. There is no real logic.'

'That doesn't mean…'

'Roger, look closer at the symbols on that ring. You see this? *This* is the Viking symbol for man, *this* for woman. Together they create *love*. Love! And with those little dots here, it's *family*. And this is all cursed.'

'Yes, but this is the common knowledge from the saga. There must be thousands of rings similar to this one. For example, the one my great-grandfather placed at the exhibition.'

'Fake.'

'Yes, but similar.'

Erica sat for a moment in silence then said: 'Yes, but unless we find Einarr, we'll never know.'

Roger couldn't fool himself. Deep inside he felt sorry for her. And couldn't explain why but he trusted her and her gut. He sighed inward and heard her say:

'The map. What did you discover?'

'It was when we followed the directions to leave the station last night. It's just a thought, but there is clearly a connection between the treasure and the Viking's grave because he was in possession of the map and Vegvisir.'

'So?'

'So, we don't have to know the exact place where he started upon his arrival from Norway, he must have had a reason to be at the place where my great-grandfather found him. Something *led* him to it. Also, there must be a reason why he died at this very spot. Did something kill him perhaps? Or someone?'

'Where are you going with this, Roger?' said Erica as she unfolded the map on the table.

'I think, we should visit the place where the excavations took place 111 years ago.'

Erica thought about it for about a second then said, 'Okay, but how are we going to do this? Didn't they just continue to build the Underground after they retrieved the treasure for the museum?'

'True. But I have this feeling, that there is a reason why Sir Roger drew all those lines symbolising different Tube trains on the original map. I think he wanted to tell us something.'

'Okay, It's a thought. Do you still have your lighter?' asked Erica, looking around in search for a pen and paper.

'No, I must have lost it.' He glanced at the unconscious Benji and scoured the ashtray full of cigarettes and joints on the table. He was just about to give up when he noticed a lighter sticking out of the sleeping man's jacket. He took it and noticed a piece of paper fall from his pocket.

He picked it up. 'Erica? Erica!' he hissed. 'Look!'

She looked. 'Shit, that's the note we accidentally left at your house.' She peered closer. 'But look, someone's tried to solve the inscription!' She looked at the figure on the sofa. 'Do you think…' she said, nodding at him. She stepped back a little.

'It was in his pocket. But nobody here knows where I live, apart from-'

Realisation dawned.

'No, it can't be. Do you really think Tony would be capable of doing something like that? With a gun?'

They thought about Tony and his eagerness to help.

'Okay, let's hurry up, before he comes back. And put the note back, so he won't realise that we suspect something.' She sat down back at the table and stared at the map. 'I think this one here—' she pointed at six o'clock '—mean South and this one—' her finger moved to the right '—East.'

'And the long inscription?' Roger asked.

'Wait.  This one could be L – U – could be either I or N – D – E or M perhaps? – I or N again –'

'– Lundenwic?' He interrupted her.

'No, no. Later we have B – U – R or maybe W? –'

'It's Lundenburg,' Roger whispered and gently ran his hand over the map. 'OMG Erica! It's the City of London!'

'Seriously? That is your big discovery?'

'No, no. You don't understand. It's the City of London! In Anglo- Saxon times known as Lundenwic but in Viking times as Lundenburg. It's not London that most people refer to as Greater London, that is built up of the 32 boroughs. The City is within that region, but it is separate too. It is the original London, where it all started. Look, it makes sense. The Romans came here, you can even still see the Wall near the Tower Hill, but Vikings were here as well. Where else to bury your hero and hide the treasure, than right in the heart of the City?'

'So, okay let's go!' Erica stood up.

‘No, wait! It’s also known as the Square Mile, which means, we would have to search 1.12 square miles. We won’t be able to do it without drawing attention to us.’

‘You could always start from the abandoned station,’ said a sudden casual voice from the sofa. ‘Where Sir Roger Wright had his secret office.’ Benji smiled up at them and winked.

Chapter 21

The young man rose from the sofa and came over to take a slice of pizza. He was taller than Erica expected him to be.

'Excuse me, what did you just say?' Erica realised she was staring at him, her mouth open.

'Hi, I'm Benji.' He smiled a cheeky smile, stretched out his hand and sat on the chair next to her. 'I work at London Underground. Secret Tours guide.' He winked at her and added, 'So I know some cool stuff.'

Erica closed her mouth, opened it, closed it again. *You are joking, right,* she thought.

'Sorry, what? You're really not making sense.' She turned to Roger, 'Secret Tours? He is kidding, right?'

Roger shrugged. Benji continued, 'You know… the ghost stations! Abandoned!' He was enjoying himself. He grabbed another slice and started listing disused locations on the Underground: 'Charing Cross, Aldwych, Euston Tunnels etc.' Roger leant back to avoid the spray of pizza.

'And you are saying… you are saying,' he began, 'that Sir Roger Wright had a secret office?'

Benji nodded.

'And it still exists?' Roger added.

'Yep. That is exactly what I am saying,' said Benji.

'And that even his great-great-grandson didn't know about it?'

Benji gave his little shrug again.

'Families, eh? Look, I can take you there if you want,' he said. He looked down at his watch. 'But we'd have to get going now, coz I need to be some place later on.'

'Take us there?' Erica's eyes were wider than they'd ever been.

'Yep. The site's closed today, so no one to disturb us. See? Cool stuff.'

Erica, unsure, thought what a nice, reassuring smile Benji had, but there was something else there…

'And… pardon me for asking,' she hesitated. 'You're not, you know, stoned, are you?'

Benji laughed. 'Nah, not anymore, but even if I was, I guess I'm your only option.'

The truth was Benji was right. And both Erica and Roger knew it. If they didn't trust him and go to check it out, they risked missing an important clue. And when all's said and done, Sir Roger really did indicate London Underground was related to the treasure. So, giving up on such a clue was not an option.

'Okay,' she said. 'Lead the way…'

'Hang on,' said Benji. He leaned over the table and grabbed another slice. 'I ain't wasting pizza. Come on.'

Brixton looked completely different by day.

Erica's head was filled with this very busy and very lively neighbourhood. Every single bar and restaurant were full. More than full. They stepped around the people spilled out onto the street as they headed for the Tube.

'Yo, man,' said a tall man walking towards them. Benji grabbed his hand, shook it, laughed, said some sort of greeting back then walked on.

'Hey, Benji, man,' a woman waved from a pavement table. Their guide waved back. People on the street passed them with a smile, wave, handshake. All happy to see him.

'What can I say? I'm a popular guy?' said Benji, catching Erica's look of amazement.

'Benji? Hey, man?' Someone looking like a younger version of himself stopped him and started chatting. He had almost as much energy as Benji.

Taking this opportunity, Erica took Roger's arm and whispered:

'Quite a character, right? Does he ever stop talking?'

Roger laughed. 'I don't think so.' He watched the funny little guide, all arms and high energy.

‘Listen,’ hissed Erica. ‘Isn’t it weird that your great-grandfather didn’t mention anything about an office? And that Benji had the piece of paper from your house?’ What she meant was: *Do you think we can trust him?*

‘Hmmm, I’ve not really had a chance to think about it. There must be an explanation, though,’ said Roger. *What might we be walking into?* he thought to himself.

Benji pulled himself away from his friend and gestured ahead.

‘This way,’ he said walking on. ‘Come on, get a wiggle on.’

Erica nodded and laughed but anyone could see she was agitated. She and Roger hadn’t really had a chance to discuss a lot of things since last night. And they barely knew each other. She tugged on his sleeve.

‘I need to know, if I can trust you.’ She blurted it out, not thinking.

‘What?’ said Roger in disbelief. ‘Me?’

Erica stammered on: ‘And Tony. And Benji.’

‘I came to you–’ Roger began.

‘For you it might be just a treasure hunt,’ Erica interrupted him. ‘But for me it’s more important. My happiness depends on that.’

Roger was confused. ‘What? Happiness?’

‘My *future* happiness. If I don’t find that other ring, I will be cursed forever.’

‘Here we are,’ Benji announced. They’d arrived at Brixton station. Erica let go of Roger’s sleeve and motioned with a jerk of her head to keep quiet. Roger thought she’d gone mad in the summer’s heat. He stepped back and let her through.

Surprisingly, the journey to the city was way shorter than Erica expected. It crossed her mind that last time it could have just seemed longer – it was late, they were cold and tired – but it occurred to her as well, that they’d just probably travelled to a different part of London. Erica looked around as they left the station. The area wasn’t familiar, but she felt a nice surprise when she realised, they were very close to that monumental white cathedral she'd seen from the river cruise ship.

'What's that building over there?' she asked pointing.

'St. Paul's Cathedral,' said Roger. 'Don't you know it?'

'Ah, yes,' she said.

'I can take you there one day,' Roger offered.

They were in the middle of central London, but the streets looked empty. A few people were sitting in the churchyard, beneath the trees, hiding from the sun. Others were quite the opposite – catching rays, lazing, the day too hot for walking around the city. It was definitely getting hotter every day since Erica's arrival. She wiped a few drops of sweat from her forehead and was just about to ask how far, when Benji announced with a hand flourish:

'We're here!'

It was a very ordinary-looking building. Red brick. Green tiles. Un-patterned. Roger looked up and down, then up and down again.

'This is, sorry, *was* an Underground station?'

Benji nodded so serious it looked like his head would fall off.

'Yes, for a very short time.' His audience did not look convinced. He stepped back and took in the building with a sweep of his arms. Time to turn on the history charm. He smiled and carried on with the story:

'You see, the late 1800s and early 1900s were the years when London Underground really developed!' Erica could hear the passion in his voice and couldn't help but be drawn in. He went on: 'But with time, they realised that some stations like Aldwych weren't really that popular…'

'Really?' she interjected.

'…Yep. Or they had to re-route the line, and so the station wasn't needed any longer, like this one.' He patted the familiar green tiles which still remained on the building and invited them to follow him around the corner. They met a gate and a padlock.

'We all know what happened in 1908, yeah?'

He grabbed a bunch of keys from his jacket, unlocked the padlock, unchained the gate and carried on with the story:

'The discovery–' Roger began.

'Yes, the big discovery,' Benji continued. 'The tomb. But after that, everybody was so focused on the treasure, that nobody ever really wondered what happened with the place afterwards. The truth is,' he gave Roger a strange look as if he was somehow responsible, 'because of all the excavations, finishing the tracks kept getting postponed. This caused delays. Eventually even though the station's building already existed, they changed the line's route. Saved time. And money.'

They reached a large metal door. He worked as he talked, flicking through the bunch of keys.

'Then your ancestor decided that if the building wasn't in use, he'd make a little office close to the discovery site. So he could examine everything. He had very good connections in the city and was very appreciated for his work. This one!' He held up a key to the light. 'No, wrong one!' He started on the bunch again.

'Anyway, the authorities allowed him to do it, under the condition that it kept a secret.'

'Why?' Erica interrupted clearly curious.

'Why?' repeated Benji. 'Cos, they didn't want to attract any treasure hunters looting or intruders wanting to search Sir Wright's office. It was all hushed up. They told the public that everything had been dug out and they closed down the station. Is it this one?' He held another key up, shook his head and continued:

'And indeed, it was a secret for many, many years. Up until quite recently to be honest. The LTM got permission to explore it.'

'LTM?' asked Erica.

'London Transport Museum. Who I work for. This station's not even open to the public yet. Not like Aldwych or Down Street.'

Roger stepped back and looked at the imposing door.

‘Fascinating,’ he said with wonder. ‘I’m a born Londoner, Sir Roger was my ancestor, and even I didn’t know about this.’

‘Ah-ha!’ Benji held up the biggest key from the bunch. ‘Gotcha!’ He inserted it into the lock of the massive door with his left hand. The doors squeaked long and creepy. Benji entered. Erica and Roger followed him inside.

The contrast between the outside world and where they stood was so vast, that it took them few seconds to adjust. Not only their eyes, but their noses and ears as well. The sun was lost behind the heavy door and for a moment they were surrounded by complete darkness.

‘Ow!’

‘Sorry!’ Erica stepped on Roger’s foot.

‘Ow again!’ he snapped.

Their guide turned on the lamps and Roger felt a little safer.

The little light switch made a huge noise in such an empty room. Once the main door was closed, they left behind the bright lights of London and its hubbub as well. In the quiet, they could hear every step they took. Every little move they made.

It’s like I’m in a horror movie, thought Erica. The orange dim light was definitely spooky, and the place stank of mustiness and rotten eggs. She felt like she was about to pass out as the air smelt so bad. But then she noticed something else. She let go of her nose, to wipe down drops of sweat which appeared on her face. Inside the station, the humidity was surprisingly high.

‘Ladies and gentlemen, welcome.’ Benji acted like he was really at work. ‘This is the ticket hall. Over there was a couple of box offices, but in case of long queues, they designed additional booth inside the lift to your right.’ He looked over at Erica, ‘Your other right. Yep, that one.’ He rolled his eyes, playfully. She blushed – she was clumsy not stupid. He continued: ‘The lift of course was never in use for public transport. Right, we have to take this spiral staircase and, after 140 steps – count ’em – we will reach the unfinished platform and the tunnel. Please hold the handrail on your way down and be careful as the lamps work only in here,' he finished and gave them one torch. 'Sorry, I have only two, so you'll need to share.'

In complete silence Erica and Roger followed Benji downstairs. Erica wasn't scared of many things but walking down 140 steps into a dark hole with two almost complete strangers hit the right note. She tried counting every step, anything but focus on how scared she was. She didn't even care anymore that she was a professional curator brought over to solve a mystery, she let Roger to go in front and gently held onto his shirt all the way down.

Before they reached their destination, they walked through a few corridors. At this point Erica started to regret not wearing anything with long sleeves, as it turned out that the temperature in that area changed drastically. It was cold and windy. The draught made her start shaking. To distract herself, she did was she liked best – research, inquiry, she asked Benji questions.

'I thought that you said, they never finished the platform only the station upstairs, that's why they decided to close it.'

'Oh darlin', ain't you never been to the London Underground before? This is not a platform; this is like maybe one third of it. Besides, as I said before, they closed the station because they hadn't finished putting the rail in, not because of the unfinished platform,' he smiled at her. He had a nice smile.

'Right,' Roger interjected, snapping a little, 'can we see my great-grandfather's office, please?' Erica had felt his shoulder tense beneath his shirt.

'Of course, of course. This way,' Benji started to walk along the platform. The guide's guests followed him and the stream of light from his torch. Suddenly the light disappeared.

'What?' said Erica.

‘Benji?’ asked Roger pointing his torch right in front of him. But there was no one there, only the wall indicating the end of pathway.

‘I’m here,’ their tour guide answered from ahead. Erica and Roger spotted the stream of light again, but this time it was coming from the level below them.

‘Careful,’ said Benji’s voice. ‘The best way is to sit down on the edge here.’ He pointed his torch at the spot he had in mind. ‘And jump. Don’t worry, it just looks higher than it actually is.’ Both of his guests followed him and stopped, a little bit shocked. Roger flashed his torch to the right, left and again right, left.

‘Where are we? This doesn’t look like an office, it looks like…’ He was just about to describe how concrete walls remind him of something when Benji interjected.

‘The Tube tunnel? Exactly.’ He hurried up an explanation. ‘The tracks that we stand on right now – these ones here – should go all the way to the next station, but you’ll see they finish not far from here.’ He used his torch again to show them what he meant. Then he continued, ‘And they start just from over there. But as I mentioned before, they never managed to finish putting rails in this place. They discovered Einarr’s grave and that was it.’ He took a few steps forward.

‘Benji,’ said Roger. ‘My great-grandfather’s office though. I can’t see anything like this in here, so what did you mean?’

‘Oh yes. I wanted to show it to you in person, but,’ he glanced at his watch, ‘I have to go. I didn’t think it would take this long.’ He looked down at the keys, thought for a moment, then said, ‘Look, Professor, Tony always spoke highly of you and even though I’ve just met you, I’m gonna trust you, yeah. Here take this.’ He handed Roger the key to the main door and added ‘Look, just follow this tunnel and at it’s very end you’ll find the office.’

‘Erm, well…’ Roger stuttered.

Erica was a little shocked. 'Benji, are you not going to be in trouble for letting us in? The site isn't open to the public yet.' She gently touched the wall's uneven surface.

'As long you're not gonna tell anybody, then I'll be alright. And don't forget to lock up.' He looked a mixture of satisfied and nervous, like he'd done his job but wasn't sure about something. Then he added, 'If for some reason anybody comes down, and if they question you, we have never met, right? You found the key. In the museum.'

'What? Who would come–?' In the torchlit gloom Erica thought Benji looked nervous too.

'Gotta go,' he said. 'I need my torch, otherwise, I'd give it to you. See ya, yeah.'

'Erm… okay' said Erica. Then they watched Benji in complete silence until they lost sight of him. Suddenly the space felt very small. Very cold. Very quiet. Erica was just about to say something again, when the silence was broken with the sound of gunshot.

Chapter 22

It crossed Benji's mind that climbing up the stairs should get easier with time. That now, nearly 140 steps will be nothing; piece of cake. But he was wrong. The fact that he struggled was simple for anyone listening to tell because, 1: the echo his footsteps made every now and then stopped, and 2: his breath was really loud. Someone could even mistakenly think that he was crying, because the water very slowly dripping from the walls in the silence was heard very clearly too. He stopped a few times and at every single step, he held his chest promising himself to quit smoking. When he eventually got back to the ticket hall, he had to rub his eyes because he was feeling a bit dizzy.

For a split second he thought that he saw someone.

'Hello?' he asked cautiously. There was no answer. He decided to carry on.

'Is anybody there?' he asked again this time hearing some sort of scratching on the floor.

He carefully walked a few more steps. Then, quickly turned around, only to realize that it was just a London Underground rat. He breathed a sigh of relief and opened heavy door which squeaked. As soon as he did it, the sun hit him straight in the eyes. He was blinded by it, so he automatically reached for his sunglasses, only to realise that they were no longer on the top of his head. Thinking *well, that's happened before,* he realised he must have left them by the entrance inside the station. He turned around and pushed the heavy metal door once again.

From behind one of the box offices, a figure in a hood thinking he was all alone, approached the spiral staircase. He slipped on the little puddle, made from water dripping down from the ceiling, grabbed the handrail to avoid falling and looked up. Someone from across the ticket hall was staring at him.

Benji had come back inside with his eyes barely open. He'd first checked the floor by the door for his sunglasses. Nothing. But he was sure he had them not that long ago, down in the tunnel in fact. It was too bright outside. He decided to look around further. As he made few more steps, the sound of splashing water drawn his attention.

'Erica? Roger?' but there was no answer.

He squinted in front of him. He still couldn't see precisely, even with the orange dim lights, and so he was not able to see who it is. Only a blurred shape who was clearly a person. It arose in front of him. Benji tried as hard as he could to see the figure's face, but not only could he still see spots from the sunlight, intruder's face and head were neatly covered by an oversized hood.

'Hey! Who are you and what are you doing here, mate? The site is closed for—'

Benji hasn't finished the sentence as the person in the hood by a speed of the light took a gun out of his back and pulled the trigger. Benji instantly collapsed on the floor and the intruder disappeared.

Chapter 23

'Did you hear that? Was that... was that a gunshot?' Erica quickly turned around and hid behind Roger.

'A gunshot? No, I don't think so. Don't be silly. How would that be possible? It's just us in here and anyway, remember? The site is closed today,' Roger answered in a calm voice.

Erica took a deep breath, steadied her lungs down. She closed her eyes, raised both hands up in the air holding the fingertips of each hand together like an exercise at yoga class to calm herself down, and brought them back down. *Okay, alright, I'm just panicking a bit. It's all good. Nobody is chasing us. It's just the two of us.* She glanced around her. *Now, focus. What do we have in here?*

She took the torch from Roger's hand and stepped away. The tunnel felt cold and scary. The end of it wasn't even visible. She had that constant feeling of an approaching train coming and running them over. This is not how she imagined dying. Apart from the rhythmic drops of water falling from the ceiling there was no other sound. But in her head, she couldn't help herself but hear the loud blaring horn of the imaginary, desperate Tube driver telling her to move from the track. It made her even more jumpy than usual. She couldn't see much either, because Roger's torch wasn't that powerful. It gave only enough light to see next few steps. And even this was not sufficient. She immediately tripped over the rail and fell on the ground.

'Ow!'

The light went out. Roger managed to quickly run over to her and help to stand up in the darkness.

'Are you okay? Give me the torch and stop messing around,' he snapped.

She blamed the bad visibility and uneven floor. She rattled the torch, then said 'Yeah, about that. I think I broke it.'

'Broke it!'

'Let me see.' Erica reached to her pocket to get her phone. 'Helvete!'

'What's wrong?' said Roger, nervously.

Erica was checking all her pockets. 'I wanted to use the torch in my phone, but I've forgotten it! I must have left it at Tony's!'

She'd heard a sigh from Roger.

'Can we use yours?' she said. 'We can't walk in this darkness. I know that after some time our eyes will get used to, but knowing my clumsiness, I'll hurt myself,' she said in such a way that Roger knew she was joking a little bit but at the same time a little bit not.

'Yes, of course.' He brought out his phone. 'Oh, damn it! Of course! It's still dead!' He shook the phone, suddenly annoyed. 'You and your story, Doctor! I forgot to charge it back at Tony's because of that!'

This was unfair. 'Oh, I am so sorry, Professor, that I happened to just find out I am freaking cursed!' Erica yelled. 'And try to turn on your phone anyway. They usually self-charge a bit while off!'

Roger laughed. He wasn't that annoyed. He tried to turn on his phone anyway. It worked indeed. 'Relax, I am joking. Of course, it's not your fault. You do know that sometimes I joke too, right?' He pointed the phone light onto his face to show her he was smiling.

'Hmpf,' said Erica.

They continued to walk in the silence. Only the sound of their footsteps echoed. Several dozen feet on and the track suddenly finished. The tunnel continued but there was less concrete, and the walls started to look rough. This meant only one thing: they were getting closer. They carried on. Some way further down they came across what they both felt was the exact place of Sir Roger's discovery. They noticed tools lying around and bits of the ground piled up.

***

The hooded figure tried to walk as quietly as possible. He realised that Erica and Roger could have heard the gunshot because in this silence sound was carried easily, but he still wanted to take them by surprise. He made his way downstairs. He had to stop couple of times, because the horrible smell of mustiness made him a little bit dizzy, but after a moment's pause, he carried on. He was determined to get them before they found the tomb first. At the bottom he worked his way to the tunnel. He entered it.

***

Erica came a little nearer to the tomb. She imagined that the skeleton of the Viking was still there. She wondered what he had been doing in that exact spot and how he died and why he hadn't been burned in the normal funeral rites. *Was he killed by Anglo-Saxons? Some mysterious creature?* Her mind ran wild. She kneeled to have a closer look. The grave looked so tiny. Roger tapped his companion on her shoulder, hurrying her up. They could always come back to look at the grave later. He couldn't wait to see one of the last places his ancestor had visited. He imagined a room full of maps, notes, some cool objects and artefacts, and tools. The thrill of maybe finding some clue left for him by Sir Roger...

Erica and Roger walked through the tunnel a little while longer until eventually Erica spotted the door in front of them. Roger pushed it. The phone torch lit the tiny room. Both, from outside and inside it looked like an ordinary old-fashioned construction site office made from wood. There was enough place for one small desk with books and papers, a chair and some tools on the floor. It must had been made in a hurry as well because through the gaps on the floor and walls the rough rock of the tunnel was still visible. Roger couldn't hide the disappointment on his face. He really thought that this would be a breakthrough. They would find something. Nothing big, but something to make them believe that they were on the right trail. That the treasure indeed exists. He could hear an insistent hissing by his side.

'Pssst, Roger! Did you hear that? I think there is someone in the tunnel. Roger!' Slight panic rose in Erica's voice. But Roger wasn't listening to her at all. She could have told him absolutely anything at this moment and nothing she said would gain his attention. His thoughts were fully occupied.

'It could be just Benji though,' she continued. 'Don't you think? Or a mouse. Yes, it's probably just nothing.'

Roger let her chatter, sniffed the dusty air and laid his eyes on the desk. Then he started to wonder if this desk was the very own desk on which his great-grandfather had written the letter to him. That was a possibility. He took a few steps forward, touched the desk surface with his fingers and sat down on metal chair. The heat and humidity of the tunnel was still palpable, so contact with something cold felt good. He put his phone on the side of little bit wobbly wooden table and started to wonder out loud: 'If I was my great-grandfather, what would I say, what would I do? I have just made this amazing discovery…'

Sir Roger put his lamp on the desk and sat down on what most people would probably describe as very uncomfortable chair. But with conditions both outside and inside, the dust and the heat, the touch of metal in his opinion actually felt really good. He took his pocket watch out and looked at the time. It was getting late. He knew that his wife, expectant with his first child, would not be happy that yet again he would be coming home so late, but he just had to know. He had this strange feeling that there was more to this tomb than the body of a warrior and a few valuable objects. He couldn't really explain it, even to himself. He just felt it. But he could find nothing.

After a minute of hesitation, he finally decided to do exactly what the runes earlier that day had advised him to do. He would write a letter to the future Wright who would succeed his generation. His great-grandson. He dipped his favourite pen in the ink well and started to write on the green custom made stationary he'd received as a gift for achievements. When he finished, he looked around at the objects from the grave. He started to wonder about their owner. Maybe it was the person called Vegvisir that the foreign students he'd met years back accidentally mentioned. His thoughts wandered further. And now, at last, he was in possession of the map. So, if this anonymous Viking was the key to the treasure and he died in this place, where Einarr should have been buried, there had to be a reason for it. Sir Wright took the map and laid it down in front of him.

'Erica, can you give me the map, please?' Roger asked, still staring at the desk.

She passed him the black tube and stepped back. He placed the burnt map on the table and said out loud to no one in particular, 'I don't understand, what are we missing?' The map looked too ordinary. 'I know that Sir Roger wouldn't have made this effort of leaving me this stuff if it wouldn't lead anywhere.' He tapped the table with his thumb and continued. 'Okay Roger, imagine you are your great-grandfather. You have just discovered the grave of the Viking. Soon after you realise it's not the one you wanted. You find a map with him, you examine the map, but it's dark, so you use the gas lantern.' Roger stared closely at the map. 'Eventually you uncover hidden rune inscriptions. So, you naturally write them down…' he finished the thought and looked up at the pile of books and documents on the side of the desk. He started to go through them. They were dusty and irrelevant until a familiar green paper dragged his attention. He grabbed it up and instantly recognised handwriting. A missing page from the letters he'd received. He was just about to start reading, when all of a sudden he felt prodding pain in his shoulder. He turned to see Erica's surprised look.

'Roger? Roger look! The Vegvisir! Look at it!' Erica held the compass in her right palm, she was using her other hand to poke him insistently. 'It's blue!'

‘Blue?’

‘I think it sense something! It looks like it has been activated or… alive!’

Roger glanced over at the glowing compass. He put the piece of paper in his pocket and stood up. He looked at Erica and said, ‘Do you – do you know what it means?’

Erica’s face was alight in blue.

‘It does mean something, right?’ said Roger.

‘It’s getting more active! Particularly over here.’ She went towards one corner of the room. And at that moment Roger’s phone died. Erica was trying to look through the gap in wooden boards when she tripped over. ‘Helvete, always, the same! What is wrong with me?’

‘It is a bit dark…’

‘Always the sa– hey!’ She discovered a gas lamp lying on the floor where she knelt.

‘Here, use this.’ Roger followed the blue glow from the compass and passed her the lighter.

She lit the lantern and brought it closer to the area where Vegvisir was particularly active – buzzing like a drone.

‘Oh, Dear Odin! Roger look at this!’ She pointed to a small symbol engraved on the rock behind the wall board.

‘What? What am I seeing? That? It looks like the Nazis’ swastika. But Nazis here? Maybe in the Blitz?’

Erica was shocked. ‘And you a Londoner? Were Nazis really down here or English people hiding from the bombs?’

‘Ah, yes. Of course. Bomb shelter. Like how they used Aldwych station.’ Roger felt foolish in the dark. ‘Makes sense. But what doesn’t is what that symbol is doing right there.’ He pointed at it.

‘I know. I know, I know, I know!’ Erica said with smile in her voice. She thought she had an answer. But the smile lasted only a second – they heard a strange sound coming from the tunnel again. ‘Did you hear that? It’s the same noise! I think it is a person! Helvete, maybe it’s the same intruder from your house!' Erica's voice rose in panic. She was a curator, not a cop.

'I don't think so,' said Roger, trying to calm her. 'It's probably Benji, relax. He probably forgot something. Like his sunglasses. Nobody else knows we're here. And only a few people have an access.' He tried to convince himself that he was right, but the hairs prickled on the back of his neck. 'Anyway, come on, hurry up and tell me about this swastika before he comes.'

Erica calmed down. 'Okay, so the Nazis took the symbol of swastika and ruined it for a lot of people. But in fact, this symbol has been very well known since like freaking forever! It exists in quite a few religions and cultures, including Norse mythology. In my country, we don't really treat it as Hitler's or an antisemitism symbol. We, as Viking heirs, believe that it was associated with the sky God – Thor – Because of this, it was often engraved on hammers and axes…'

The compass was going crazy, as if it was trying to get through the wall.

'Hammers?' said Roger. Erica nodded. 'Here, try this' Roger handed her a hammer from one of the tool bags in the office 'I think if Vegvisir is going so crazy in this exact spot, there must be something behind that wall.'

Erica shrugged, passed him the compass and grabbed the tool without hesitation. She started to smash the wall. Thud! Thud! She noticed she enjoyed this activity. It felt nice. She also realised that, quite unintentionally, she was picturing Bjørn and Matilde kissing in front of her. She started to smash the wall even more effectively.

It didn't take long to make a hole and then a rudimentary passage. They crawled through only to discover that it led to a cave. They stood in the new gloom, lit by Vegvisir. Then they heard a crashing noise. The entry they used was now gone. Their passage had caved in.

Chapter 24

Erica stared at the pile of stones. Her eyes kept blinking, like this would magically change the picture she saw. The passage leading back to Sir Wright's office was really gone.

'Helvete,' she hissed. Then thoughts ran through her head: *How are we going to get out of here? What if we'll run out of air? What if something will attack us.* She paused thinking of next horrible possible thing to happen. *What if* – she stopped a second later and shuddered. Her eyes widened. She nearly dropped the lantern. Roger was watching her closely.

'Erica? Erica! Hey, what's wrong?'

She didn't say anything, just pointed at two huge, looming figures to the right of her.

Roger laughed. 'You do know that these are just our own shadows, right?'

Erica sighed with relief and said, 'Phh, of course I do. I just wanted to scare you! You know, for a joke?' In the gloom, she imagined Roger didn't quite believe her. 'Anyway, can you give me the Vegvisir?' she said, nonchalantly turning around so he wouldn't notice the slight blush of embarrassment on her face.

She couldn't see much, but she had a feeling that wherever they were, the place was quite big. She took a few steps forward. The sound of distant echoes confirmed that it wasn't small space. She kept going barely able to see where but following the glowing compass. There was a change in the temperature as well. The humidity was gone. She couldn't feel any draughts either but sensed it was cold. All of a sudden, she felt a vibration in her hand. She glanced down on her palm. The compass was shaking. It looked like it was ready to fly away.

'Roger? Roger!' she squealed. 'What's happening to the compass?'

‘Oh, another joke, Doctor?’ Roger ignored her and continued examining the collapsed wall. He was trying to find out if the passage they just used was gone for good. ‘I don’t understand this. I mean, how is it possible?’ he stared surprised at the pile of rubble in front of him. ‘Yes, you used a hammer but are you *that* strong, Dr Skyberg?’ He turned around and realised that Erica was nowhere close.

‘No, for real.’ She held her hand as far away from her body as she could. ‘What is happening with Vegvisir! Look at it!’ The compass made little noises which started to scare her. She carried on walking quickly.

By the time Roger had caught up, she was quite far down the tunnel. Then she screamed because she’d run into something.

‘What the hell?’ it took her a second to realise what was in front of her.

‘What? What is it?’ said Roger.

‘I believe,’ she hesitated, excited. ‘I believe it’s a fire pit.’ She finished the sentence with slight confusion in her voice.

The temperature seemed to drop even lower here. They both shivered. Erica decided to go with the impulse. She smashed her gas lantern right in the middle of the pit.

‘What did you do that f–?’

It worked. A sudden bonfire lit the cave, which in fact was way smaller than they expected. Erica looked around. To her right she spotted water pouring down the ceiling and walls in tiny waterfalls. In the good light from the fire, she also noticed a sort of giant picture stone right in front of them. It was carved in limestone. It looked like the kind of ornate slab of stone that used to be very popular among Vikings. There was an inscription on it, but not visible enough to read. Erica swore under her breath, then spotted that on one side of the slab were attached two wooden torches. She came closer, took one of them and made her way back to the fire.

'Here, hold this,' she said to Roger and gave him the compass.

Erica shoved the torch into the fire. It lit instantly and made her jump a little. She walked back to the picture stone. Now it looked like it was playing a role of gate or door. She stood in front of it and said out loud to herself: 'I wonder what's behind it. Einarr's tomb? Nah, that would be too easy. Maybe it's a trap and some mysterious creature will jump on us?'

'Are you able to read this inscription, Dr Skyberg?' Roger interrupted her monologue. Erica looked at him and said, 'I'm not sure, I can't see much. Let me get a bit closer to it, maybe then I'll be able to make sense of it.' She took a few steps forward.

'Dr Skyberg!' In Roger's hands the compass was buzzing. Frantic. 'Look, the Vegvisir is going really crazy right now!' he shouted. 'We have to figure out how to open this gate!' Roger struggled to hold the compass in his hands.

Erica turned around to see what all the fuss was about. She was standing so close to the slab that she accidentally brushed it with the torch. Within a second, she felt heat on her back. She turned around again. The entire wall was on fire.

'Oh helvete,' she whispered in a surprisingly calm voice (with just a slight note of fear in it). Then she yelled, 'Roger, look!'

They stepped back and watched the flames very carefully. It didn't take long for the fire to settle down. Now, it clearly showed the whole engraved picture on the slab and the runic inscription around it. Straight simple lines forming the shape of a tree and a string of letters above it:

ᛁᚠ ᛃᛟᚢ ᚲᚾᛟᚹ ᚺᛟᚹ ᚹᛖ
ᚹᛖᚱᛖ ᛞᛁᛊᚲᛟᚹᛖᚱᛖᛞ ᛃᛟ

ᚢ ᚹᛁᛚᛚ ᛒᛖ ᚨᛚᛚᛟᚹᛖᛞ ᛏᛟ ᛖᚾᛏᛖᚱ ᚦᛖ ᚲᛁᛏᛃ ᛟᚠ ᚱ ᚢᚾᛖᛊ

Erica stood with her mouth wide open. Even though the cave was quite hot from the fire, she had goose bumps. The flame showed nine lines, some of them with additional smaller branches. She knew this. That all together it was meant to represent the always-verdant tree. On each of the lines, at different heights, was an additional very simple picture which looked like a tiny planet with runic symbol in it. In the middle of the tree was an image of the squirrel *Ratatosk*, and below it three roots which came from three primary springs: *Urd's well, Mimir's well* and *Hvergelmir*, with the dragon *Nidhogg* gnawing the roots.

'What is that?' asked Roger, amazed.

'It looks like Yggdrasil, the Tree of life in Norse mythology. It connects nine worlds, you see?' she pointed at nine images around the lines which made up the picture of the ash tree.

'Excuse me, what?'

'You know, *Asgard* where Odin and rest of the gods lives, *Midgard* where we human belong, *Alfheim* the home of elves–' She was interrupted from listing all the worlds by the fire. It sizzled. Pppfzzz. Then she could have sworn she saw a rune coming up from it.

'Did you, did you see that?' she gasped.

'What? Sparks coming from the fire?' Roger answered, surprised by her question.

'Sparks? Oh, just sparks?' She really could have sworn… 'Never mind.'

Roger pointed at the wall. 'Erica? Inscription on the door, please?' He was getting impatient.

Erica Skyberg turned back to the image of the tree. She acted like a child at Christmas 'Whoaaa, this is incredible!'

'Yes?'

'It says: *If you know how we were discovered, you will be allowed to enter The City of Runes.*' She thought for a moment then said, 'City of Runes? Of course! Vikings, Vegvisir, Einarr, Völva, symbol on my cursed ring – everything lead back to the runes!'

'Do you know how we were discovered? And who is "we"?' Roger said. '"We" as in runes?' He turned to her hoping she could help, he knew she was an expert but… 'Do you know the origins of *these* runes?'

'Do I?' Erica laughed, excitedly. She closed her eyes and began to recite:

'Veit ec at ec hecc vindga meiði a netr allar nío, geiri vndaþr oc gefinn Oðin…'

Roger sighed. 'Erica, I don't understand what you're saying. The most Norwegian I know is "helvete". And that's because you keep saying it!'

'Oh, I'm sorry, let me translate it.' She started to recite from the beginning: *'I know that I hung on a windy tree nine long nights, wounded with a spear, dedicated to Odin, myself to myself, on that tree of which no man knows from where its roots run.'*

Roger tried to listen, he wanted to, but his attention was being dragged away by the compass. The vibration was growing stronger and the blue disc was feeling hot now like it was about to burn hole in Roger's palm. 'Something is happening!' he hissed. Using both hands he tried make it stay put, but with every passing second, he had to struggle more. The Vegvisir was behaving like a little drone helicopter, trying to fly away. By being forced to stay, his engine was boiling. Roger fought to keep it calm and in place. Erica, conscious of things happening, tried to ignore him and continued: *'No bread did they give me nor a drink from a horn, downwards I peered; I took up the runes, screaming I took them, then I fell back from there.'*

She had barely finished speaking when the door slowly opened, the last line of the poem was the key. She and Roger stood, hesitating. Roger was still struggling with the compass and for a moment he looked like a man possessed by supernatural forces. When the door had fully opened, the compass was so frantic he had to give up.

'Hey! Wait! Where are you going?' Roger yelled after the compass. 'Erica! The Vegvisir! It's just flown away!'

They looked after the compass – a flying drone zooming off through the door. The energy from behind the door seemed to give it power to fly. As if it moved using power from the runes. Then it zoomed back, and circled Erica and Roger. It was teasing them and at the same time inviting to follow it inside. It zoomed off again.

Behind the door was quite dark. All they were able to see was a flying blue dot with eight vectors, which spun around and around. On it, runes glowed brightly. Erica grabbed the other wooden torch, lit it and gave it to Roger. She took a deep breath and stepped inside.

***

The hooded figure watched the passage crumble up ahead. He ran. But he was too late. When the noise of the stones had settled, he could hear chattering from the other side. He took out his phone and prepared a text, then a few more, ready to send them when he reached the surface again. He turned back. He was angry and disappointed.

Chapter 25

Erica walked through the door. This was the City of Runes. The name alone made her heart skip a beat and her body feel electric with excitement. She held the firebrand out in front of her. Her eyes were wide open; ears prepared to hear even the softest sound. Her body tensed. She was ready for whatever was about to happen. She took a moment to think: *Isn't it weird that I have never heard of the City of Runes? And what is this place exactly? It doesn't look like a city, not even an ancient one. Does it mean that somehow the runes live here? Are alive? But how?*

Roger broke her thoughts.

'Where did the compass go?' he whispered behind her. As soon as he stepped through the entrance, the stone door closed behind him. 'Not again! Great, now we *are* trapped,' he added looking nervously around.

'*Now* we are trapped?' said Erica. 'So, before when you were staring at the massive pile of rubble you still thought we had a chance of going back that way?' she asked with laughter and added, 'Roger this might be good! Exciting! This can only mean that we are on the right track to the treasure!'

'Or to death,' he said with sarcasm in his voice.

The tunnel wasn't big. There was enough room for them to walk freely but it was not as big as the one leading to Sir Wright's office. The temperature was still cool, but with so much going on, they barely noticed it at this point. Because of the size of the place, the light from the two torches was enough to have a better look at the space.

'What is this place?' Erica said. She gently touched the uneven, slightly wet wall. 'Did Vikings make it? Or your great-grandfather with his crew?'

Roger followed her gaze. 'I am not sure. It's too small for the Tube tunnel though. It could be just a passage leading off somewhere. Check the map, maybe there is a clue.'

Erica slowed. 'Ha-ha, very funny.'

'What?'

'I don't have it. You have it,' said Erica in very serious voice.

'Hey, stop messing around.' Roger brought his torch closer to her face to check if she is smiling or not.

'What? You were the last one with it, Professor. You were examining it on the desk! Are you telling me you *left* it?' She took a deep breath and continued, 'You have a habit of this! You left something yet again as we had to leave in hurry because someone was chasing us!'

Roger stammered, 'The V-Vegvisir distracted me! There was no time to think straight!'

Erica swore, 'Helvete! I didn't even have chance to finish translating the inscriptions from it!'

'Look, I'm sorr– wait a minute!' Roger grabbed the familiar green piece of paper from his pocket. 'Here. I found it among my great-grandfather's notes.'

Erica took it from his hand. She carefully examined it and was just about to start to make sense of it, when suddenly the Vegvisir appeared again. It started to fly around her head. Automatically she started to bat it away like an annoying bug. Then in a split second, she changed her mind and wanted to catch it. She chased it. Every time she was close, it escaped. 'Roger, help me!' she snapped. They followed the glowing blue disc for a while until they reached a chamber where the tunnel was splitting into three. In the wall above each entrance there was a single runic word.

'Where now? Which one shall we–' Roger hadn't finished the sentence when suddenly the Vegvisir rose up to the ceiling and turned itself upside down. It looked like it was waiting for something. Neither Erica not Roger could reach it. It seemed to have stopped now. Erica paused and checked if it was going to move again. It gave her the opportunity and time to focus on the notes from Roger's green paper.

It didn't take her long to figure it out. 'Coordinates! These are coordinates! I kept looking at them as letters, that's why it didn't make sense!' She said it so quickly and so excitedly that she nearly run out of breath. She continued, 'This could be the coordinates for the exact position of Einarr's tomb. Yes, that's possible–'

'Look, it's another fire pit!' Roger shouted. He barely had touched it with his wooden torch when the flame roared. The blaze was so high, it tickled the ceiling. To where the Vegvisir hovered.

Erica ran over. In silence they watched the Vegvisir start to shake then it fell down straight into the middle of the fire.

'Roger! Helvete, I need it!' Without hesitation she put her hand into the flames trying to reach Vegvisir. The fire was too big. She started to explain, 'I was just about to put those encrypted coordinates into the compass, into Vegvisir. I can bet it would lead us directly to the tomb!' She watched the flames dance. 'I can't believe this is happening!' She closed her eyes and rubbed them with one hand to make herself calm. 'I will be freaking cursed forever. That's it. I will die alone. There is no hope for me. The more I fight, the more…'

'Erica, calm down.' Roger took her shoulder to comfort her. She looked at him in resignation.

The fire pit sizzled. She turned around and wanted to come a bit closer but before she managed to make a move, the fire started to flicker and leap. She heard the sounds of small explosion few seconds later.

'What the hell!' Roger took a few steps back. 'Are these? Are these… runes?'

They watched as sparks from the fire formed into individual fireballs. Each fireball with rune in them. They started to fly in different directions. After another second another explosion. A slightly burnt Vegvisir landed at Erica's feet. Some of the runes from around its disc were gone. So was the fire pit.

Chapter 26

Benji opened his eyes, not really knowing what was going on around him. He blinked once, then a second time. Wanted to raise his head but as soon as he attempted it, a formidable lady ran over to him and ordered him not to move. He was in such pain, he didn't even argue. He passed out.

Benji opened his eyes again. This time a crowd of onlookers, paramedics and police were there as well. He was still lying on the pavement. This time his head was on someone's lap. It was the same lady. In a calm voice she was telling him that she was a nurse and everything would be alright. He couldn't remember what happened. Had he been involved in some accident? Did someone rob him? He held his head a bit higher and looked down his body. There were drops of blood on his T-shirt.

'Excuse me' he croaked at the lady with effort 'Am I, am I dying?'

'No, of course you are not. You will be fine. You're just in shock. The police want to talk to you. Do you think you'll be able to answer a few questions?' The woman waved at someone in the distance.

Benji didn't answer when a ginger-haired gentleman approached him and knelt down.

'Hello, I am Detective Charles O'Sullivan. Can you tell me what your name is and what happened?'

Benji managed to sit up and lean his body against the wall. He touched his head. It felt like someone was smashing something inside it. He looked up. The familiar green tiles signalled to him that they were still outside the abandoned station. Yes, there was a gunman! He'd nearly been shot. As he wasn't saying anything, the detective continued:

'Listen, a few witnesses said they heard a gunshot. Shortly after they saw you crawling from behind this…' indicating the metal door.

Benji looked at the man's stern face and immediately realised that he was the one suspected to be the gunman. He freaked out. 'Oh no. You got this all wrong, Detective. My name in Benji. Benjaamin Anderson–'

'Benjaamin,' repeated the detective, as if not believing him.

'It's Hindi,' said Benji. 'I was giving a private tour to two friends of mine.'

'Hmmm, yes. And exactly how long have you known Professor Wright and Doctor Skyberg, if I may ask?'

Benji was amazed. 'H-how did you - how do you know I was with them?'

The detective smiled a little bit smugly. 'Simple. They missed an important meeting at the museum stating they had a new clue into the incidents there. They mentioned you.' He did not look happy.

'But I swear, I didn't do anything!' Benji wailed. 'Someone took a shot at me!'

'Hmmm… And you are lucky they missed and you only have a mild concussion.'

Benji started to say something, but at the exact moment Tony appeared at the scene.

'Hey, Benji, what happened! Where's the professor and Doctor Skyberg?'

'Oh,' asked Charlie getting his pen ready to take notes. 'So, you know them as well. Who are you?' He looked at Tony like he had looked at Benji, with suspicion.

'I'm Tony Miller, Professor Wright's personal assistant.'

'His PA?' asked the policeman. 'I don't think we've met. I'm assigned to the museum's incidents.'

'I've not been in much since then,' Tony said. The policeman made him nervous. 'I left the professor and Dr Skyberg at my house today. Then I got a text from Benji saying to come here.'

'*I* messaged you? I don't remember that.'

'There you are guys! I have been looking for you!' Suddenly from within the crowd Tony's sister appeared. She looked like a female version of her twin brother.

'Hey, Annabel. Where did you come from? I just came from that direction and I didn't see you,' Tony asked his sister with clear surprise in his voice. 'Anyway, what on earth are you doing here?' he added, then, 'Hey! That's my hoodie! I told you to ask me before you took my stuff! By the way, isn't it too hot to wear that?'

The detective stepped in. 'Not wanting to break up your family reunion but we're here for a reason,' he said.

Annabel smiled at him then turned to her brother; 'Where did I come from? I got a text from Benji,' she said, waving with her phone. She completely ignored his other questions. Everyone on the street looked at the guide waiting for an explanation.

'He probably doesn't remember a thing,' said the nurse. 'I think someone took a shot at him and missed. But he collapsed and hit his head against the floor.'

'Yeah, I am with the nice lady,' said Benji. 'I didn't do anything!'

Charlie O'Sullivan glared at him. 'Are you all telling me that a gunman might still be inside there and that Professor Wright and Doctor Skyberg have no clue that they are in danger?' he asked, irritated at such irresponsibility from the guide. The policeman acted quickly. He took his gun out, headed to the door and, before anyone realised, was gone.

'Oh shit, man, you're right! I left them down there!' said Benji. He paused and held his aching head in his hands. 'Where are they? The tunnel is not that big!'

'What if. What if…' Annabel started, but Tony shushed her. 'Stop it, sis. I'm sure that Erica and Roger are fine!'

There was a noise in the crowd. They spotted an elderly lady who crossed the police line in a hurry. She ignored anyone who tried to stop her. She was unusually fast for a woman with a walking stick. A stick she even used to threaten a policewoman who tried to stand in her way.

‘Leave me alone or you’ll regret it!’ She waved the stick in the air.

‘Excuse me, madam, you cannot be here. Only witnesses and people helping with inquiries,’ another of the police officers said as he managed to get to her.

‘Do I not have a right to know what has happened?’ she wailed. Everyone looked at her with curiosity. She was a mad woman talking nonsense. ‘Where are they? Where are they! Someone mentioned a gunman. Where is the gunman? Do something!’ she swiftly swept over to Benji.

‘Tell me where they are. You seem to know this place.’

‘The truth is,’ said Benji. ‘We don’t actually know. Sorry, but who are you?’

‘Oh helvete,’ she said. Then she fainted.

‘Hello, ma’am?’ Tony laid the old woman flat on the pavement next to the tour guide.

His sister stepped up and pushed him out of the way. ‘Madam? Madam, wake up!’ Annabel grabbed the elderly lady’s legs and held them up. Then she checked her eyes and heartbeat. Tony had never seen his sister so worried about someone, especially a stranger. He was just about to ask why she is so interested in this woman, when Detective Charlie O’Sullivan reappeared.

‘Right, there’s nobody inside. We followed the tunnel until the end. Even that small passage at the back of the office,’ he reported.

‘Yeah,’ one of his Scotland Yard colleagues added without thinking if it was confidential information or not, ‘there was just a pile of fresh rubble. Looks like they went into the passage and the wall collapsed.’

‘A cave-in?’ someone said.

‘What?’ said Benji. ‘Are you saying they might be dead?’ He was in such shock that he nearly jumped up.

The detective stopped glaring at his colleague and glared at Benji. 'There is still hope. Did you say your name is Anderson, as in *the* Anderson family?'

'Yes,' said Benji. 'Mayor Anderson was my great-grandfather, why?'

Charlie ignored him. 'And you said you were giving Professor Wright and Doctor Skyberg a private tour?'

'Yes, I've followed my family's footsteps and became an expert on this city. I'm a secret London Underground tour guide. Why?' asked Benji not really knowing what Charlie had in mind.

Charlie carefully pulled out slightly burnt map from under his jacket. 'You see, we found this on the table down there in that office and wondered if you could make any sense of it.'

Benji sat up straight again and took the map to see closer. After a short silence he said, 'I can maybe make some sense of the Tube lines, but I don't know what this is' he pointed at inscriptions. 'This looks weird. But…wait a minute. I found this piece of paper in my jacket. It has something similar!' He reached to his pocket.

'Those look like runes,' said Tony looking over his shoulder. 'The old Scandinavian alphabet. We have quite few objects with Anglo-Saxon runes at the museum.' He sat down next to Benji and leaned in. 'This here ᚾᛟᚱᚦ could be an N, then a letter I don't know, R, TH. Oh so it could be just North or something. This here ᚹᛖᛊᛏ W, next one is E, something and T, could mean West then.'

'There's a lot you don't know,' said Charlie.

Tony glared at him and continued 'But this and this,' he pointed to the individual squares with runes, 'they don't make any sense. It almost like they are not letters, maybe perhaps they're…'

'Coordinates,' said a suddenly croaky voice. The old woman pulled Benji's left arm out of the way to get a clearer view. 'These aren't letters, these are numbers.' She tried to sit up.

'Who are you?' Charlie looked down at her. She looked back, with a glint in her eye.

'Greta. Greta Skyberg. Erica's grandmother.'

Chapter 27

Erica and Roger were still somewhere in the underworld of London. In the City of Runes.

The Vegvisir lay at Erica's feet. It was not moving. Little wisps of smog floated in the air making impression that the compass might want to cough. Erica did not take her eyes off it. The longer she stared at it, the more she felt her heart breaking a little bit. The Vegvisir looked like it just lost his soul. Its blue glow was barely visible. She put the still blazing torch down on the floor and carefully picked the compass up. As it had just come out from the fire, Erica expected it be really hot but surprisingly it was the opposite. Cold like a stone. Cold like it was dead.

She looked around for Roger. She wanted to show him Vegvisir.

'Roger? Roger, where are you?'

'I'm here, I'm here!' his voice came out of the tunnel. 'I tried to follow one of the runes. Man, they are fast!'

Erica looked miserable. 'Roger, look, the Vegvisir. It looks like it's dying.' Erica held it flat in her hands. It was not moving. She noticed some of the runes from around the disc were missing. She wondered if that could be the reason why it stopped working. If the runes were its power supply then without them it won't work. She murmured to herself, 'I'm not sure. It could be…' She hadn't finished the sentence when around her it went dark.

'What just happened?' she said.

'Erica, I believe the water coming from the ceiling just put down your torch!' Roger tried to light the fire pit and her torch with his own torch, but they were too wet.

Helvete! Erica thought. She took her torch. The fire was gone. She peered into it a little bit closer. Only the small light from Roger's torch remained, so she had to try quite hard to focus in order to see something. Erica didn't know why, but she had a hunch that there was more to that object than it looked.

She started to examine the top of the wooden baton, but then hesitated: *What if the fire suddenly comes back to life. I'll burn myself?* She kept waving her hand back and forth, then eventually closed her eyes and slowly, carefully, tapped it. On the top of the burnt wooden baton, right where the fire had been just a second ago, was carved the exact shape of Vegvisir. Without thinking, she placed the compass there. She didn't know what was supposed to happen. Nothing did.

She fiddled with it for a few seconds until a quiet click announced that the compass perfectly matched with the shape. Instantly, bright blue crepuscular rays came out of the compass. They were pointing in the eight Nordic directions of the world. It looked like a spiritual awakening. Rays of enlightenment. God's fingers. Erica squinted in the brightness. She held the staff so close to her chest, that she was forced to push it away. Her arms were full of tension. Pain was burning through the muscles. She banged the torch on the floor. Erica's hands were shaking. She banged it on the ground again. On top of the now staff, Vegvisir started to spin around like crazy, but not in a way that it was losing control; it acted like was a toy. A whirligig. She held the staff with both hands, struggling to keep it still. Then, she hit the floor one more time. She felt she was losing control of it, yet she didn't want to let it go. Suddenly, a wind rose from all four tunnels. A whirlwind. Roger who stood nearby, was nearly knocked down. The wind created a central column, a tube like a hurricane. Erica was right in the heart of it. It didn't hurt. And she wasn't afraid. She just kept looking around, up and down. Just waiting. Suddenly unknown voices started to whisper. It seemed that they were coming from inside the whirlwind, but she couldn't see anyone. The language they spoke, she couldn't quite understand either, apart from one phrase she'd known since childhood. It was in Old Norwegian. Without knowing why, she started to repeat it over and over again: *Du kommer til destinasjonen selv om du reiser sakte. Du kommer til destinasjonen selv om du reiser sakte…*

The wind still spun around her, faster and faster. It didn't make her feel dizzy. It was just cold. She shivered. The staff felt cold as well. Erica thought how it was weird because the light coming out looked like rays of sunshine, but they felt icy. The light from the Vegvisir shot blue in all directions but the compass was still. Suddenly, she noticed she was rising slightly up into the air like an invisible force lifting her. Holding the wooden baton, Erica now spun in the opposite direction to the whirlwind. The unknown voices became louder and louder. Then a mysterious shape formed from the wind and a hooded character came out. She started to walk around Erica.

'What is happening to me?' Erica screamed.

'Don't be afraid, dear. You are not in danger. How can I help you?'

'Who are you!'

'My child, do you not know me? As far as I am aware, you asked for me.'

'*I* called you? How? This all happened by itself!'

'Did you use your staff to knock on the floor three times? Did you say: *You get to your destination even if you are traveling slowly? Du kommer til destinasjonen selv om du reiser sakte.*'

'I-I guess so. Yes! I don't know!' Erica was still shouting, but the voice of the figure was calm, quiet.

'My name is Hertha. I am Völva. The Reader of Runes.'

'Völva? You? Y-you're the spirit of my ancestor, Hertha?'

The figure nodded.

'Wait a minute, you are the one who created that curse in the first place!'

The figure nodded again. 'Please, tell me, how can I help you, my child?'

Erica didn't even need to think. She said, 'If you were the original creator you must know something about this city, about the tomb, perhaps how to lift the curse?'

'Of course, but first things first, my child. Vegvisir was created here in the City of Runes. It will not work unless complete. You must find all of the runes and bring the Vegvisir back to life. Once you know what to do, it will lead you straight to Einarr. Find your inner Völva, Erica, and follow your heart.'

Suddenly everything around Erica turned faster and faster and after few seconds the whirlwind and shooting rays were gone. She fell onto the ground, still holding the wooden staff. Vegvisir attached on a top of it. Silence and darkness filled the room. She shivered. The floor was cold and damp.

Roger was quickly by her side. He helped her to get up.

'Are you okay?'

'Nnngk,' said Erica. Roger was just about to ask what happened when something familiar looking very like a fireball rune exploded at the scene.

Chapter 28

'Excuse me, madam, did you say you are Doctor Skyberg's grandmother?' Charlie looked at the elderly lady with clear interest.

They were all still gathered outside the abandoned station near St. Paul's. Greta made a move to stand up and Annabel quickly offered her help.

'It's okay, it's okay. I'm fine, dear,' Mrs Skyberg said. She took the young woman's offer of support anyway. 'Thank you.' She nodded at girl then let go of her arm whilst looking for her walking stick. Annabel picked it up from the ground where it lay and handed it to Greta. The woman gave her a slightly stern look. 'You are very kind, but please don't ever touch my staff,' she quickly winked at her before anyone else noticed. Annabel smiled shyly.

The sun was going down, as it was done for the day. With it, the heat was gone as well. The sky changed from clear blue to grey. Clouds appeared, and it was going to rain any second now. The paramedics and most of the police where gone from the scene too. It was just the five of them: Benji, who it turned out was absolutely fine and had played a bit of drama queen before; Tony and Annabel, Detective O'Sullivan and Greta Skyberg. The four Londoners stared at the map, trying to understand what the old woman was talking about.

'Coordinates? Numbers? Aren't runes the ancient Scandinavian alphabet?' Tony questioned Greta. She blinked slowly, smiled sweetly and said:

'Yes and no. You see, young man, runes are mostly known for being letters or special symbols, but Vikings and rest of the ancient world needed numbers as well. As they didn't like to complicate their life and wanted to have it as simple as possible, they just nominated runes to be a number from one to nine. So, naturally, quite few of them are repeating, but this just made everything more exciting for the foreseeing world. Especially that they have included the blank rune called Wyrd, which simply means fate.' She started to mark numbers on a disc on the top of her walking stick.

'Oh man!' said Benji. 'You've got a compass on top of your walking stick? Are you for real?' The old woman smiled again and nodded at him.

'Yeah, what is this?' Tony joined. 'Wouldn't be easier to use the phone?'

Mrs Skyberg looked at them shaking her head with silver hair. 'You, young generation. And how will you use your phone in the middle of the forest or far up in the frozen north? Your phone could die. Your phone could have no service. With my compass, I always know where to go.' She said it with such a confidence and warm voice, that nobody dared to question it.

As everyone watched Greta enter the coordinates, Benji remarked 'Hey, I think I've seen Erica with something similar.'

The old woman had trouble to hold both the piece of paper and the stick.

'Here, I'll help you,' Annabel offered. She grabbed the note and stood in front of Greta.

'Okay, let's see what do we have here.' Greta started to translate the runes to coordinates:

51°30'57''N 00°05'31''W

'North West?' said Benji. '51° – 0°? If I am not mistaken, I believe it's still here in the City of London.' He took the map from Annabel and carefully studied it as he followed the underground lines. 'It will be between St. Paul's, Bank and Moorgate if I am not mistaken.' He started to walk.

'Let's go,' Charlie ordered the rest of the group. 'Before it gets dark.'

Tony turned to Benji. 'Are you sure you are able to walk?'

'Yeah, man. Don't worry about me. I wouldn't miss this for the world. Besides, if it's pointing to another station, you'd better have me with you.' He winked at Tony and his sister.

Greta stepped in front and led the way. The four turned around and one by one followed the silver hair leader. A few passers-by stopped every now and then to watch this unusual picture. Even with the variety of London, watching an elderly woman using her walking-stick-like metal detector wasn't something ordinary. The group passed by St. Paul's Cathedral. Then turned left, left again and continued straight on. When they reached Gresham Street, they passed by St Lawrence Jewry, then right across the square, the familiar municipal building of the Guildhall grew in front of them. White with its several pointy towers, reaching skywards. Perfectly blending in. They approached the entrance from the library side, just to find out the door was locked. A note pinned to the window said: 'Closed: Private Function'.

The whole group sagged. 'What now?' asked Tony. 'We can't leave Doctor Skyberg and the Professor somewhere underground on their own! We still don't know if there's someone after them. Detective, please do something!'

Charlie looked around and spotted a security guard outside the wooden door on the other side of the square. He took out his badge from the inside pocket of his suit and approached the man. After few minutes he gave them signal to join him.

'Right. There's a private event going on in the crypts for 200 people right now. We are allowed to enter but under supervision of one of the Guildhall employees.' As he finished speaking, the guard kindly opened the door for them. A very young, smiley lady met them. She introduced herself as Cornelia. Charlie saw that Greta was not happy about the company.

They stopped in the Great Hall, waiting for Greta's instructions. When she moved, they moved. When she stopped, the immediately stopped as well. The whole group followed her to the end of the corridor until they reached a staircase. A sign directed visitors to the crypt. They waited for a gaggle of tipsy people, were clearly enjoying themselves and looking for the smoking area, to climb the stairs then they made their way down.

The place was dark with flashy disco lights. They found themselves straight onto the dancefloor full of drunken people. Greta ignored them and started to turn around following the compass. It was directing her to the corner of the crypt by the window.

'It's here,' she whispered to herself. 'Einarr's tomb is somewhere here.' Her eyes sparkled. The rest followed her until she stopped. 'It is somewhere under here!' She pointed with the stick on the spot on the floor.

They all looked down at the beautiful parquet. 'But how we are going to get there? We don't have any tools,' Annabel asked, concern in her voice. Greta Skyberg turned to Charlie. There was something strange and edgy about her.

'Detective, clear the space,' she commanded. 'Stop this party and take this people out, so nobody will be hurt.'

'Excuse me?' said Charlie.

'Was I not clear?' she glared at him. He looked confused – why was she ordering him about?

'What do you mean hurt?' Tony interjected. 'Why does anybody have to get hurt?'

The old woman turned on him like a tiger. 'Do what I say, now! Why are you arguing?' But within a second Greta's tone changed. 'Ah, excuse me. Where are my manners? Naturally I'm worried for my granddaughter.'

'Oh, come on, relax, people. I am sure we can get some kind of—' Benji hadn't finished the sentence when the fire alarm sounded.

Within seconds, chaos and panic filled the room. People were screaming, running, pushing one another to get out. The five were alone. Charlie went to talk to the fire brigade. It was a drill, he'd said. There was no fire. It took some convincing. He told the Captain they were working on very serious Scotland Yard business and they couldn't leave. He wasn't happy, but he could see there wasn't a fire.

As soon as everything had calmed down, Greta followed her compass to the exact spot by the window, raised her walking stick and, nodding once at Annabel who closed her eyes, banged it against the floor three very powerful times. All of the sudden the tiles on the floor cracked wide open. A bright blue light shot out when everybody was forced to step back, covering their eyes, blinded by the light, Mrs Skyberg stepped forward. She took Charlie's gun from his holster.

'Annabel, dear, make sure nobody follows me.' She handed the gun to the young woman and stepped in the blue tunnel, leaving everybody in blind shock.

Chapter 29

Erica took Roger's hand and quickly stood up. Hertha was gone. The hurricane was gone. So were the eight rays coming from the compass just a moment ago. The only light now came from Roger's torch and the very quickly approaching ball of fire. It looked like the image of a horse was formed inside or, as it came even closer, a horse galloping out of it.

'Watch out!' Roger screamed and Erica jumped out of the way, avoiding direct contact with the fire by inches. She looked at her shoulder. It was hot. She wasn't burnt but still few sparks caught her T-shirt. *Ufff, that was close!* she thought.

The horse disappeared in the tunnel.

'I don't get it! What happened to the runes? How am I supposed to find them if they don't exist anymore?' She started to walk in circles, talking nervously out loud.

Roger stared at her. 'Erica, what are you talking about? What happened in that whirlwind?'

'Hertha, the Völva who created the curse, the rings, everything. She said I need to collect all the runes and bring Vegvisir back to life. But how I'm gonna do that if—' Another fireball tore down the tunnel, this time in the shape of bow.

'If what?' asked Roger.

'If they have changed into those weird shapes! Let me think. Vegvisir loses some of the runes, therefore its power. Runes are escaping from the fire and coming back as fireballs with images of things – a horse and a bow…'

'Why a horse and a bow?' said Roger. 'Such random objects. Could they represent anything, like you know horse because Odin had one, bow because… I have no idea,' he added, flatly.

'Yes! You are right, Roger! Oh, I could kiss you! Odin had *Sleipnir*. But his horse had *eight* not *four* legs.

Hmmm, but let's stay with the idea it's all connected. The rune ᛖ *ehwaz* or rather *eoh* in the old Norwegian divination system means horse. Yes. And look! That is one of the runes missing on the compass disc!'

'Okay, so that's easy. We should catch those fireballs somehow, name them by recognising the shape and place them in the heart of Vegvisir. How about the bow then?'

'I must say, it's a tricky one. The problem is that with so many available sources each book names the runes and what they represent a little bit differently from one another. I believe that Vikings could call rune ᛇ *yr* a yew-tree, but I have seen it translated it as protection as well.'

'So, which one of the missing ones is it? Where will we place it?' asked Roger looking at the compass.

'Oh helvete,' Erica said quietly. 'It's this one right here.' She pointed at a glowing rune.

'I don't understand. I thought we are collecting missing ones, so how come this one is already here?'

'Roger, I don't know. Let's focus though.' Then, totally against what she'd just told Roger her thoughts wandered a little... 'We have been here quite a while, though. I wonder if anybody even noticed.'

'I don't know,' said Roger. 'But yes, as you said, let's focus.'

Erica turned around and entered the tunnel where the last fireball had disappeared. She tried to perceive which exactly were the missing runes, but the light from Roger's torch wasn't enough. This she realised only few seconds later was a good thing because another fireball not that far from them was now clearly visible. It stopped as if it was waiting for something. Erica, under the influence of adrenaline, started to run. She left Roger without a word and just ran. Thoughts were speeding through her head, all concerned with her future happiness – *Only by catching those runes I will ever be loved. Will I ever have the chance for a real relationship. But how do I catch them? I can't touch them with my hands. The fire will burn me.*

She noticed the staff in her hands. *Wait a minute, I don't necessarily have to touch them. What if I'll use this?* She hadn't finished the thought when she realised that the rune was about to move again. She wasn't close enough yet to reach it.

It was not going to get away.

Unusually for her, it took Erica only a second to decide what to do. She took a swing and threw the staff like it was a javelin. It travelled far and fast down the tunnel and hit the fireball straight in the middle. The image immediately got sucked inside the compass and the staff dropped down on the ground.

Erica had shot off so quickly, that Roger was still lagging behind. When he finally managed to catch up with his companion, he ran over and picked up the baton. Erica and Roger looked down at the disc. The ᚹ rune appeared right in the middle of Vegvisir.

'Hah. How about this one? Wait a minute, it looks the same as Anglo-Saxon rune *Thurs*. So, if we put it right here,' he said proudly and moved the symbol to the right spot on the disc. But the Vegvisir wasn't happy. The staff started to shake and spat the fireball back at them. It just rejected it. By the time Erica and Roger could react, the rune was long gone.

'Roger!' yelled Erica. 'It was rune *wynn* ᚹ not *thurs* ᚦ! How you could confuse *joy* with *troll*? And look, now it's gone!'

'Oh shit! You're right. I don't know what to say—'

'Just let me handle it–' Erica started to say.

Roger hadn't even got to apologising when a fiery horse appeared not far from where they were standing. They started to run after it. As soon as Erica was in a straight line with the fireball, she threw the staff again. Bullseye! This time the rune ᛖ was visible on the compass's display. Erica quickly moved it between ᛒ and ᛗ. They waited in suspense. After a second, *ehwaz* started to glow in blue.

‘Yes! Okay, so we have four more to go.’

‘Another one!’ Roger snatched the staff from Erica’s hand and skilfully sucked fireball in the shape of droplet. He picked it up and came back to her.

‘Droplet,’ said Erica. ‘Interesting. It could be… oh, I know. It’s ᛚ *laguz* which means *water*. Definitely.’ She moved the symbol with confidence.

After a second or so, a familiar blue glow signalled she was right. Everything was now happening very fast. They hadn’t even had a chance to discuss the last rune when two new ones emerged. The chase had begun. Roger run towards them and again hit one of the fireballs right in the middle with his first attempt. When he turned around, he realised that Erica had stopped halfway through and was trying to catch her breath. He didn’t know what to do. She was too far back to go and consult the symbol and the second fireball started to disappear.

‘Catch the other one before it’s gone!’ Erica shouted in panic. God, she hated running.

Roger had no time to argue. He just ran. The symbol of the *gift* grew closer with every step. The curator quickly judged the distance and with all his power threw the staff.

‘What is it? Show me, show me!’ Erica caught up with him and took the Vegvisir in her hands. She moved ᚷ *gebo* to its place and asked, ‘Where has the other one gone?’

‘It was right there! Shit! Maybe it doesn’t work like that and we have to do them one by one. Sorry, I didn’t know what to do! I didn’t even have chance to look what was it. I’m sorry.’

‘We already lost one! We haven’t seen it again. What if they won’t be back? What if we’ve lost our chance?’ Erica sat down on the ground. The vision of not finding Einarr overwhelmed her. She covered her face with hands and repeated over and over *‘detter skjer ikke, deter skjer ikke’* as if it was a mantra: ‘this is not happening, this is not happening’.

‘Erica? Erica! I think this is our lucky day, look!’ Roger grabbed her hand and pulled her up.

They ran. They ran without thinking where or for how long. There were tired and hungry. And they didn't even realise that they were now running on the tracks. They saw two lights in front of them. Yes! The two remaining runes. But then they heard a familiar sound approaching them. It was a Tube train coming straight at them.

Chapter 30

Erica and Roger ran along the tunnel. The two lights in the distance quickly grew bigger and brighter.

'Wait a minute. Shit! These lights don't look like fireballs anymore. What the hell?' said Roger in panic.

'No? But it must be something!' Erica answered full of hope. The wind coming from the other end of the tunnel caressed her face. It reminded her of the whirlwind and Hertha.

'Erica, it's a train! It's a freaking train!' All of the sudden Roger realised what was going on. Erica was lost in her thoughts, thinking of what her ancestor had said, but suddenly the word 'die' brought her back to the tunnel and the lights.

The wind coursing through the tunnel made their bodies shiver and fire from Roger's torch gone. The air wasn't cold. Quite opposite. But the realisation of what was happening caused goose bumps to appear all the way from their hands up to their back. The hair on their heads danced chaotically. Erica kept brushing her hair off her face as she ran, although for a split second she thought that maybe it would be better to not see what was about to happen. The train approached with speed, not giving them a lot of time to think. Erica suddenly stopped.

'What on earth are you doing!' Roger started to slow down but kept running. 'Look up! There is some kind of ladder on the ceiling going throughout the tunnel!'

Erica glanced up. 'Even if there is, it's too high up! We'll never reach it! There's no point going back, and clearly the driver hasn't even realised that we are here! So why should I run towards it? To speed up my own death?' She watched Roger getting smaller and smaller. *If only I could get the driver's attention. If he could only see us, then maybe...* She looked down at the staff she was holding. She started to wave it over her head, hoping to get the driver to notice them. But the light coming from the runes on the disc wasn't nearly powerful enough. Judging from the distance between them and the Tube, the driver would still have a chance to avoid the catastrophe, but he was not even trying to stop, totally unaware that he was about to run them over. Erica screamed at the top of her lungs, but wheels banging against the rail made such a racket, there was never a chance for the driver to hear her.

Then she was struck by another idea. With no further waste of time, she detached the Vegvisir from the staff and quickly reattached it again. It had worked before. It really had. She wasn't even thinking she could lose the runes again. All she cared about was to be alive. Even if that meant she was still cursed she would be cursed and alive. *Last time I did it, those powerful blue rays shot out of it. Let's hope it will work again. May all the Norwegian Gods be with me right now.* She jumped into the air. As soon as the compass found itself back in the right spot, exactly what she had prayed for happened. Powerful blue light, like God's fingers, brightened the tunnel.

Seconds later her relief forced out the air she held in her lungs. Thousands of sparks lit up under the train. It had worked. The driver had noticed the light. He immediately yanked the emergency brake, praying out loud to stop in time. He didn't even know what the light was or where it was coming from. But it was clearly in his way. The sparks flew out and the train made very loud creaking noise as it slowed. But it had not yet stopped.

Erica watched it coming closer with every second. She was so busy being terrified, thinking that at any moment she would lose her life, that she hadn't even noticed what happened to Roger. The light from Vegvisir didn't spread far, so she couldn't even see where he was or how far away from her he was. And the train still came. Erica stood straight, frozen like a rabbit in headlights. She held staff the same way a Viking warrior would hold his weapon willing it to protect her. The light from Vegvisir weakened, then was gone. She closed her eyes and focused on the warm air that still caressed her face. She waited for the worst to happen. She waited for her death.

Any second now. Any second now.

Erica suddenly felt her body rising. She opened her eyes and looked up. She couldn't see anything at first but heard Roger screaming something whilst lifting her up by the staff. She intuitively grabbed it tightly and let him pull her up. Then she could see. He was hanging upside-down whilst holding the gantry with his legs like it was a trapeze. His shirt had slipped down, almost covering his face. Out of habit, her eyes quickly scanned his muscular body as he grabbed Erica's hand and quickly tugged her up. She clung onto his waist and climbed over his body onto the gantry above the tracks. As soon as she could sit down, she helped Roger to get up. Just in time.

Not even a second later they saw and felt the thunder of the train grinding the tracks right beneath them. Erica, relief and fear pouring over her, lay down and clenched the gantry bars with one hand, the other held her staff. She closed her eyes, still afraid. The gantry was shaking. She was scared she was going to roll off. Roger seeing her slipping, threw himself over and covered with his body. He clasped the metal bar of the gantry keeping them in place and watched the Tube as it slowed down.

It seemed to them that everything lasted forever. But eventually the train stopped. In the strange quiet, Erica and Roger opened their eyes and watched the driver get out his compartment. Although he wasn't far away, the Tube stopped way further down than where Erica had been standing not that long ago. Roger had saved her life.

'Are you okay?' Roger whispered in Erica's ear. She felt hot and sick, and his body was heavy on top of her, but she nodded, yes.

'Good.'

And because she couldn't think of what else to say she said, 'Thank you.'

Roger wanted to laugh. 'Oh,' he smiled in the darkness. 'Erm, you're welcome.'

They were right above the train, so neither of them could see what was happening to the poor commuters inside. Even so, they didn't want to hang around to find out.

'We should get out of here. I don't want them to ask what we are doing here or need to explain the light from the Vegvisir,' said Roger. Erica nodded again and slowly turned her head around. Their faces were inches from each other. They could feel the heat. They could hear their heavy breaths. See each other's eyes.

***

'What the hell?' the driver squinted into the tunnel. 'What the hell is that?' He noticed a searing blue light up ahead of him. He was just about to pull the emergency brake when started to panic: *What is this? I've never seen anything like this. Could it be a terror attack? Quick, Bert, remember the training? Maybe better not to stop, then? Or what if it's organised crime? Mafia? Shit! But it's flashing? And how comes it's so powerful? Maybe something happened with the rail. Shit. What to do? What to do!* Bert Perkins had never thought so quickly in his life.

'Ladies and gentlemen, this is a quick announcement. Please hold on to the handrail and secure yourself as there is something on the track and I am forced to stop this train immediately.' He switched the button to pull the break hard. 'Once again, there's no need to be alarmed but please hold on to the handrail. There is an incident ahead of us. I will get back to you, once I have more information.' Bert forgot that when you tell people not to be alarmed, they'll be alarmed. He could hear shouting in the cabins behind him, see people on his little monitors getting angry.

The train started to slow down. Sparks from under the wheels limited Bert's visibility. He quickly grabbed his radio and contacted the control room at Bank station. They had no idea of what he was talking about. Cold sweat flooded his back. The train slowed some more until it ground to a stop.

'Ladies and gentlemen, this is your driver again,' Bert said, a little bit distracted. 'Thank you for staying calm. Errrrm it seems like, it seems like the train, yes, that's it, the train has broken down at the next station. There is nothing on the tracks, that information was wrong. Please, stay in your seats and wait for further instructions.' But Bert didn't sound convincing and the train full of weary Londoners started to complain to each other. Suddenly the light inside the carriages went out and the complaining changed instantly to panic.

***

Screams filled the Tube train as the passengers inside panicked. Erica and Roger could hear them banging on the doors, trying to break out. The two quickly decided to use the opportunity to flee the scene, so when the driver flashed his torch in their direction, they were already gone.

Roger quickly and skilfully crawled along the gantry, like a monkey in the Zoo. Erica tried to keep up with him as best as she could.

'Pssst, where are you going?' she hissed.

'There must be a station not far from here,' Roger answered.

'Hell no!' Erica disapproved of his decision. 'We have to go back and catch all the runes!'

'Back?' yelled Roger.

'Yes!' yelled Erica.

'You're insane!'

'Cursed!'

Roger stopped in his crawling tracks. Erica could see his body sag.

'Okay then,' he said. 'Give me a moment. I need to get our bearings. When we ran to catch the runes, we must have accidentally taken a few wrong turns and exited the

City. I think we ended up somewhere around Bank, which is tricky even to change from the Central to District line. Believe me, I know. I do that commute often.'

Erica ignored the last comment and said: 'How do we get down though? How did you get up here in the first place? It's really high!' She leaned out and looked down. The tunnel's emergency lights were giving just enough of a light to see by.

'I followed a hunch, knowing that at some point there must be some kind of emergency ladder on the wall. And it would reach this gantry. I was lucky to find it on time, because running towards an approaching train, I admit, wasn't the smartest thing.'

They crawled for few minutes until Roger noticed another ladder on his left. He climbed down, grabbed the staff from Erica and helped her to get back safely to the ground.

'Thank you.'

'You said,' said Roger.

'I mean it,' she said. 'If it wasn't for you, I would be long…' She stopped mid-sentence. She was staring down the tunnel right behind him.

'What is it?' Roger tried not to panic. 'Is it another train?'

'No,' gasped Erica. 'The runes are back!' She quickly glanced down at the compass.

'Roger, we're missing only two runes: ᚹ *wynn* and ᛁ *is.*'

Roger followed her gazed and dodged a fireball rushing straight at him. 'But Erica?' he grunted, 'why are there so many of them?'

She looked around the tunnel. There were dozens of fireballs flying straight at them.

She dodged a particularly large one. 'Quickly!' she yelled running in the other direction to avoid contact with the fire. 'What images can you see?'

Roger quickly scanned the fireballs as they approached them. He dodged few of them again and said 'Cattle, a sun, a cartwheel, a snowflake—'

Erica answered right after him: '*feoh, sigel,* cartwheel will mean journey or riding so rune *rad*, a snowflake… a snowflake?'

'Yeah, thick one, could be made of—'

'Jackpot! Made of ice!' She scanned the area and spotted the fireball she wanted. She touched it with the staff. The symbol was sucked in and the rune ᛁ appeared in the middle of the compass. She quickly swiped it to the spot on the disc right next to *gebo*. The symbol glowed blue for a second – it's in its right place. 'Right, one more!' she yelled.

The runes had already moved away so they had to run again. Roger shouted to her as they ran: 'What's the last one? What am I looking for?'

'The last one is *wynn* which means *joy.*'

'How the hell am I supposed to know how *joy* looks like?' He looked at his companion in confusion.

'I don't know! Just focus and tell me what you can see.'

They'd slowed down a little, the fireballs in front of them. 'Okay, I see a home, some sort of Goddess, a tree and another tree, a bow.'

'Wait a minute, you see two trees and a bow?' Erica asked with curiosity. After spending so much time together, Roger knew she had some sort of lead.

'Eeee, yes, why? What are you thinking?'

'Something isn't right, Roger. The trees can symbolise runes: *yr* which means yew and *beorc* which is birch. But then *yr* could be a bow as well, so bow would act as a *weapon* made from wood, not as *protection* as I thought before. That leaves us with–'

'Could for some reason *joy* be a tree?' asked Roger, thinking it was a very stupid thought and wary of the earlier joy/troll incident.

'Wait a minute, you are right! You genius! *Wynn*, is joyful harmony but the symbol itself, you know the one you accidentally confused with troll earlier–'

'Yes, I remember,' Roger snapped.

'Well, in many sources it looks and is linked to the tree, or rather the *fruit* on the tree. It symbolises the fruition of hard work in the divination system. Hard work, Roger! This must be it!' She ran over with excitement and quickly touched a fireball before it disappeared. The runic symbol ᚹ lit up the middle of the compass. Erica's heart was pounding so fast, that even Roger thought he could hear it. She knew, that as soon as she moved the last rune, the disc would be complete. That Vegvisir would regain its soul. The curse, she was sure, would be lifted. She clicked the last symbol into place and waited for the blue glow. She watched the compass come back to life.

The eight blue light beams shone in the darkness. Erica nearly dropped the staff. She fumbled in her pockets and quickly retrieved the piece of paper Roger had found in his great-grandfathers' notebook and entered the coordinates. Vegvisir started spinning so quickly that after only a few seconds the individual beams, the god's fingers, disappeared and the compasses dial was lit by familiar blue glow, as if it had sucked all the rays of light inside it. The Vegvisir rose up into the air. It made few circles around them, as if it wanted to show them that it was back to its strength. It started to slowly fly away.

With the fireballs gone, the compass was the only visible light. Erica grabbed Roger's hand, 'In case you trip in this darkness,' she added, and he didn't take it back. They followed the compass in silence, hoping that it would take them to Einarr.

Chapter 31

Erica and Roger chased the friendly blue light for quite a while. It reminded them of a toy drone controlled by a child. Every now and then it made unnecessary circles or acrobatic numbers like figures of eight. It made no sound, although Erica could have sworn that she heard it saying 'weeeeeee' several times. They had no clue exactly how long they walked for, but in the cold and darkness they silently wished it would end soon. With every turn they felt the tunnel becoming weirdly smaller. *It must be a trick of the dark,* Erica thought. She touched the wall. Concrete and brick now turned to rock. *So no, not a trick of the dark*, she said to herself. It really was getting smaller. The corridors became shorter, so Erica naturally felt like she was going through a maze. Couple of times they had to run in order to catch up to the Vegvisir and not lose their flying guide. As the time passed, they noticed the ground getting muddy and a few rivulets of water appeared under their feet. They glanced at each other and silently agreed that water in tunnels wasn't that unusual.

The blue light ahead hovered in the darkness.

'Hey, it stopped. I think it's waiting for us.' Erica let go of Roger's hand and pointed at Vegvisir in front of them.

Roger missed the warmth and slipped his hand into his pocket. He noticed a wall indicating the end of the tunnel. 'Or maybe there is nowhere to go,' he said.

They came over to the compass a little anxious. They had already been wondering around down there for several hours and had absolutely no idea how to find their way out. So, if it flew away or they lost it, they'd probably face certain death. But the glowing compass stayed where it was. By the tiny blue light, Erica noticed a familiar symbol on the wall.

'Hey!' she said. 'This must be it! Look at these triangles!'

Roger looked at it. 'Is it the same symbol as on your ring?' he asked.

'No! This is *Valknut*! And because they usually appear on graves, I can bet that Einarr is behind this wall!' Erica jumped with excitement. Roger was stunned for a second then said:

'First of all, excuse me it's a *what*? A walnut? And second, are you telling me that the tomb is behind this wall?' Roger tried to push the wall in case it would move. 'But how are we going to get there?'

'Leave it be, it's probably protected by spell.'

Roger backed away and wiped his hands as if that would help.

'Let me think for a second,' Erica said. She touched the symbol and started to think out loud. 'Valknut, not walnut by the way, is a Viking symbol associated with death. It is a graphic image of three interlocked triangles. It means—'

'—Knot of those who fallen in battle,' Roger finished for her, then continued, 'I have seen it before. On the Anglo-Saxons cremation urns we have at the British Museum. I didn't know they had such a strong connection to Norse mythology. Although, when I think about it now there are quite a few images of wolves and horses on those urns and they were usually alongside Odin, right?'

Erica was a little impressed. 'Yes, that is correct. And look, the symbol is surrounded by runes. Exactly the same size as around Vegvisir. It makes sense. Didn't your great-grandfather tell you in the letter that Vegvisir is the key?'

'Yes, he did! You're right!' He quickly grabbed the compass out of the air just above them and placed it on the Valknut, making sure the runes covered each other. It fitted perfectly.

Erica and Roger stepped back, both holding their breath and waited for something to happen.

And waited...

After a minute or so they looked at each other with clear disappointment in their eyes.

Erica walked over to the wall and tapped it. ‘I was so sure, that we were right! The symbol has a right meaning, Vegvisir is exactly the same shape. And yet nothing! What are we missing, Roger?’

‘Maybe we didn’t collect all of the runes? Or maybe we damaged Vegvisir when it fell into the fire pit? Or perhaps, we should use something other than the compass,’ Roger started to think out loud.

‘No. It can’t be it. Your great-grandfather used the word *key*. He definitely said that *Vegvisir is the key.* We must follow that direction. If it’s a key, it should open the door. But this door has no handle. Or at least I can’t see any.’

‘To be honest, I can hardly see anything,’ added Roger. ‘Only that blue glow from Vegvisir. It’s as if it wants the whole focus to be on it.’ He touched the compass. The disc moved. ‘Funny. You were right at my house; it does feels like the combination lock to a safe or something.’

‘What did you just say?’

‘I said. Funny. You were right at my house, it does feels like–’

‘Oh, Roger! I know what you said. That’s it! I forgot about it! We need a password to access the tomb! We need to show the City of Runes that we are worthy to find it.’

‘Excuse me, what? *Show the City of Runes we are worthy?* Erica, are you not going a bit too far with all this? Maybe we’ve just hit a dead end.’

‘Too far? Too far! We followed a flying compass. We chased freaking fireballs in the shapes of runes. I spoke to my dead ancestor!’ she said. ‘Yes, with all that has happened today this indeed sounds crazy!’ Her voice echoed through the tunnel. ‘But it’s important!’

‘You’re right. I’m sorry. I guess…’

‘For you it’s all about the treasure,’ Erica continued. ‘You don’t even know what exactly is in there. But I know. It’s your treasure but it’s my *happiness*. It’s my only way to lift the curse, don't you understand? The fact that you are single is your own choice, Roger. You meet girl after girl, and it's your choice to not get attached. With me–'

'What? Attached with you?' stammered Roger.

'No,' said Erica, '*with me* no matter how much I like someone, I know, I will always be alone. And that isn't my choice.'

Roger looked at the floor and said, 'I know, I'm sorry. I guess I have a minor concussion after that fall I took to avoid this one fireball. I don't know what I'm saying.' He gently touched his head.

'What fall?' Erica was suddenly worried for him.

'Oh, nothing.' Then Roger said, 'Fireballs. Do you think it was a coincidence we had to collect those particular runes?'

Erica stared at the wall. 'Could be. Or could be not. Do you think they mean something put together?' Erica was in her own world, now, just thinking out loud. 'We had: *wynn* which disappeared, *ehwaz, laguz,* we lost one I don't know which one, then we had *gebo*, *is* and *wynn* again. So, if we lost *joy* but it appeared again, I think we lost the *ice* rune before.' She looked around. 'I need to write this down.' She still had the green piece of paper, so she turned to Roger. 'Do you have a pen?'

'No, I don't, sorry.' He started to think in a bit of a panic about how he could help her now. For some reason, he really wanted to make up to her for his previous faux pas.

'You could use your staff on this muddy bit of ground here.' He pointed down by his foot. Erica knelt and wrote down: ᚹ ᛖ ᛚ ᛁ ᚷ ᛁ ᚹ - w e l i g i w.

'What does it mean, Erica?'

'Absolutely nothing.'

'Oh, but if we caught them in no particular order, then would that matter? Would it make any sense if you switched the places of some of them?'

'*Elig, welig, ewig*? No, no, no. But wait a minute. What if *w* is actually the letter *v*? Einnar was a warrior, so after death he went to Valhalla.' Erica's brain worked quickly. With every second, with every idea, she felt, that she was getting closer to an answer. 'Everybody who goes there, lives in afterlife. And we can swap this and this and we have: ᛖᚹᛁᚷ ᛚᛁᚹ. Yes. Yes! That's it!'

'So, what does it mean?' asked Roger.

Erica rose up and started entering the combination into the compass. 'It means: *Evig liv*. Eternal life.' She took a few steps back and watched the disc and the eight staves spinning around in two different directions. After a few seconds she and Roger heard a *click* and saw the familiar blue crepuscular rays streaming out of the Vegvisir once more. Then the light disappeared. As soon as it did so, the stone in the wall marked with the symbol started to move sideways. The entrance appeared.

Erica and Roger looked at each other in wonder. The tomb was pitch black inside. They hesitated.

'What now?' Roger caught himself whispering for some reason.

'Hey, look!' Erica pointed inside the dark hole.

The darkness started to grow brighter and brighter. As it was as if the Vegvisir had just heard them. Within seconds, twenty-four fireballs emerged in the air and one by one flew to twenty-four wooden torches fastened to the wall around the room. Erica and Roger silently walked in. Only the sizzle of the fire and the echo of their footsteps was heard. The place looked like a small chamber.

'Look at this!' Roger felt like he had just walked into heaven. He ran towards the nearest objects and started to name everything he picked up. 'Shields! Axes! Coins! Swords! Brooches! Everything is here! The whole treasure is here!'

But Erica's attention was directed to something completely different. In a middle of the chamber, on a pedestal, was the burnt wreck of a small ship and what looked like the remains of a body. She came closer and circled it, paying close attention to everything. She noticed the familiar-looking ring on Einarr's right hand. She looked at hers, then back at his, smiled and thought: *Finally. This is going to change my life.* She stretched out her hand and lifted the ring from the bone that was once a hero's finger. She placed it on her own finger, right next to the ring her gran cursed her with years ago. She waited in suspense. All her hopes and dreams were about to come true. No more loneliness.

But nothing happened.

'I don't understand,' she sobbed. 'Why nothing is happening? I don't understand! I thought that by having both rings, by putting them together, something magical would happen, Roger. And the curse would be lifted!' Erica Skyberg sat down on the ground and hid her face in her hands. Tears started to pour.

'We don't always get what we want, my darling,' said a croaky voice behind her.

Chapter 32

Erica uncovered her face.

'What? What are you doing here!' she said.

Roger quickly looked over at the entrance to the tomb. 'Who are you?' he asked, thrown by the appearance of a body in the doorway. He slowly picked up one of the axes from the floor.

'Someone, who is more important than you, Professor Wright' came the reply. 'Erica, darling, is he always so nosy?'

'I am serious. Who the hell are you?' He grabbed the axe in both hands, ready to use it.

'She's my grandmother,' said Erica, her voice angry.

'Your–'

Greta Skyberg looked at Roger with contempt, murmured something in a strange language, pointed her walking stick at him and just like that his body collapsed to the floor as if some invisible power had just knocked him down.

'Roger!' Erica by the speed of light found herself next to him. He looked pale. She held the unconscious body of her companion 'Roger? Roger! Can you hear me?' She shook him with all her strength. He didn't wake up. Erica turned to her grandmother.

'Why did you do it, Gran? What has he done to you?'

'Oh, my dear! What have I done! You must trust me. I didn't mean to! He just didn't want to stop asking questions…' the old woman smiled.

'What are you doing here and how did you find us?' growled Erica.

'Oh honey, I've missed you! I felt bad after our phone conversation and decided to find you,' she said in a saccharine voice, ignoring the fact that her presence in England was weird. 'I was worried about you and wanted to explain the whole situation with the curse and the ring in person. It wasn't right to have it over the phone.' Greta's eyes stopped at Einarr's body. They twinkled. Erica followed them.

'I don't believe you, Gran. You're clearly capable of doing things I never thought you would. How could you do this to me! You cursed a child!'

'I understand you're mad. You must have so many questions! And I'm here to answer them. I am here for you, honey.' Greta slowly took a few steps forward, but more in the direction of the body than her granddaughter.

Erica looked at Roger and said 'Look what you did to him! Don't try playing all nice now! Who are you trying to kid?'

It was as if Greta Skyberg suddenly changed into a different person. 'Oh okay, you're right. Who am I trying to kid? Just give me the rings, Erica.' She stretched out her hand, her tone of voice sharp.

Erica was astounded. 'Is that why are you here? For the ring? Wasn't it enough to curse me and my mother? Who's next on your list?' Erica felt furious, but somehow, she managed to hold it in. 'Who are you and what have you done with my grandmother!'

'Don't be stupid, Erica. Not just for Einarr's ring. For both of them. I thought it was clever that I got the girl to steal the ring from the museum when it went back on display, but once I found out it was fake, I was so angry, Erica. And then, quite by chance your young professor,' she pointed to the floor, 'called you up with a marvellous story about Einarr's real tomb. The Gods shone on me that day. So, give them to me. Now!' Greta raised her walking stick. She was losing her patience. She knew that the longer she left Annabel upstairs alone, the more chance somebody would find them and the tomb.

'You stole the ring?'

'Not me exactly.'

Erica stood still in the chamber, not able to move or speak. It wasn't often people saw her speechless. Her usually always open mouth was now firmly closed. She tried to process information she just heard. There were so many questions: how? what for? why? WHY!

'How, how could you?' she finally said, stuttering. 'You, you are the one behind events at the British Museum?' Her eyes glazed. She tried to hold back tears.

'Now, my child,' Mrs Skyberg replied.

'I am not your child! Or grandchild! From this moment we are not related at all. Do you hear me? AT ALL! I just wish to understand, Greta. What is so important about those rings for you? What can be more important to you than human life! Than your own grandchild being happy?' A few tears rolled down her cheek again.

'The guard's death wasn't planned. It was just a stupid mistake someone working for me made. But we human beings tend to be selfish, you know? And this is me putting my happiness above anyone else's. Give me the rings! How many more times do I have to ask?'

'No. I need those rings and you know it. You know this is the only way to lift the curse – the curse you cast on me!' Erica's voice started to break. 'This is the only way for me to ever find love!'

'Don't be ungrateful,' Greta spat. 'I raised you. I took you under my roof. Into my arms. Even though you were the one who killed my child! I fed you. I even listened to all this whining about your unhappy love life. Now, Erica, it's time for you to pay me back.' She pointed with her staff at her granddaughter.

'Or what? Huh? What you are you going to do?' Erica wasn't afraid. She knew deep inside, that if Greta wanted to hurt her, she would have done the same to her as she had to Roger. She wouldn't stand here, arguing. She might not know her as well as she thought, but she knew her well enough.

'Do you really want to argue how much those rings mean to me?' said Greta in a threatening voice.

Erica tried to understand. The fact that her grandmother was behind everything was a great shock to her. She clearly wasn't the woman she'd grown up with. Yes, she had trusted her more than anyone in the world, even after their last phone conversation, but this? Erica knew there must be a good explanation for her grandmother's behaviour.

'Help me understand,' she said. 'Why go through so much trouble for this. Why do you need them? What is so special about them?' Erica noticed a hammer among the treasure and picked it up. She placed the rings on a stone altar slab. 'Maybe neither of us should have them? They clearly don't work anyway.'

Greta gasped. Seeing the hopelessness on the face of her granddaughter, she knew the child was neither joking nor bluffing.

'The seeds!' she yelled.

'The what?'

'The seeds. Inside each ring are two seeds. They are last of their kind, so if you destroy them, no one can benefit from them.'

Erica looked at the rings. 'What are you talking about? There are no seeds in here. You just made that up.'

Greta stepped forward a little. Erica raised the hammer. 'Erica! Do you remember the story my mother would tell me? When in the saga Einarr went to Hertha to cast the spell?'

Erica nodded.

'There is more to it,' and Greta started to recite:

'With the rings in his hand, he remembered Hertha's prophecy about the plague. He travelled back into the woods to ask Völva to cast a spell on the rings: whosoever owns them, will be protected against all disease.'

Erica was just about to stop her, as this wasn't anything new, but, hammer poised, something told her to wait a moment. Her grandmother continued:

'Seeing them engraved with symbol of love, Hertha decided to hide in the heart of the rings four seeds. The last of their kind, they would be used to make an antidote for the coming plague. And because they were the last of their kind, they soon would be gone forever.

Hertha disguised the seeds as precious gemstones. She added two to each symbol on the ring. "Now, my lord," she said, "I have gifted you with the symbol of family. The gemstones will change colour every time you and your Beloved think of each other."'

Erica looked at the rings again. Indeed, both of them had two gemstones each. She looked closely and thought she could see a tiny pip in the centre of each one.

Her grandmother hurried with the explanation. 'Einarr was so miserable and in such pain, he never asked Hertha how to lift the curse. He was so sure that he'll never need to. But she saw in the casting of the runes, that one of her descendants would be cursed. And she knew that plague was coming. She decided that an antidote made from all four seeds would either cure illness or lift the curse.'

'Curse or cure?' said Erica. Greta nodded. 'Are you ill, Granny?' Slowly Erica started to feel awful, maybe she had jumped to conclusions and was so focused on herself that she didn't think about others.

'No, dear, not me.'

'I still don't understand.'

'When your mum wanted to marry your dad, I was angry and lonely. I wanted to curse her just for a short period of time. Just to get rid of him. And I knew I could break the curse when he left. But she died giving birth to you. She died before I managed to fix it. And I guess wanted to deny the fact that it was my fault, so I blamed you.'

Erica shook her head silently. 'So, you knew that I was cursed all my life? And how to lift it? Why you didn't do anything?' she sobbed. She felt betrayed. She felt lonelier than ever.

'Over time, I wanted to. I would need to find the other ring, but I had an idea about where it was. But then I met someone.' Greta finally put the staff down. 'Like you, I grew up without a mother, as well as you know. Father was so distant it was as if he didn't exist anyway. I lost your grandfather. Then your mother. And when there was no hope for happiness, I met someone. Felt alive again. Felt loved again.’

***

Greta Skyberg had just put her granddaughter down for the night. After making sure that Erica was asleep, nice and cosy, Greta sat on the patio in her house in Oslo with a beer and crossword. But something wasn’t quite right that October evening. She couldn’t focus. Wanting to find out what was wrong, she looked to the runes for the answer. No matter how many times she tried, that evening, the stones had only one rune for her – ᚱ *Raido. Journey.*

‘The Runes wants me to go somewhere,’ she said out loud. Her sight stopped to one of the words on the crossword. The answer was ‘Svalbard’.

The next day Greta went to the coffee shop in the city and asked her daughter’s dear friend Sofie to take care of little Erica for a few days. Three hours later Greta was on a flight to the Island of Svalbard. When she arrived, it was already dark. At her hotel the receptionist informed her, ‘The sun this time of the year here in the Arctic Circle, is up for about to four hours. Around 10–14. That makes it the perfect spot to watch Northern Lights.’

She got Greta’s attention. ‘Where can I book a guide tour for it?’

‘Everything is closed for today, but you can go to the tavern. All locals and tourists gather there every day, so you can ask around.’

And there she was. Far away up North in the Norwegian snow, looking for a tavern. Not even knowing that behind its door, she would shortly meet someone who would change her life forever; that inside this pub, would be a scientist having a pint of beer after a long day’s fieldwork, where he worked with his crew to discover how the changes and impact of global warming affected the environment. She had no idea that he would be the one to make her happy again.

***

Erica listened to the story. Something about it rang true. 'But you never mentioned him,' she said. 'And besides, how does this have anything to do with me being cursed?' She started feeling sorry for her grandmother. She put the hammer down and came closer to her. She could see tears in the old woman's eyes.

'You were too young to tell you about him, and when you grew up a bit, I still held anger towards you for your mum's death.'

'And now?'

'Why mention him now? You see, Erica, they made a discovery not that long ago. I told Mathias that he should retire years ago, but he wouldn't listen. He wanted to do something good for the world. For next generations. A discovery you might have heard of in the news quite recently.'

'What discovery?' Erica tried to think. 'Wait a minute, there was something about discovering bacteria frozen in the ice hundreds of years ago. That there was a rumour it caused plague in Viking times and it could come back due to the climate change. They never really gave description of it though.' Erica remember the news she watched in the hotel. 'Was it just a few days ago?'

'That's it! So, my Mathias was the one to discover it but at the same time he was exposed to it. He's in a medical centre in Svalbard. They are running tests, trying to find out how to cure him, but it doesn't look good. But I know that Hertha's antidote can help him! And I know how to make it. He has maybe three days left if we don't act now.' She wept openly. 'Erica, honey, I really don't want to lose him. I know I am old, and, in your eyes, I don't deserve it.'

Erica looked at her grandmother with a broken heart. She was torn. She could save somebody's life, and the life of the woman who had raised her, or for once in her life be totally selfish herself and lift the curse.

Erica's grandmother was sobbing and leaning on her staff. The same staff she'd used on Roger. Her granddaughter picked up the rings from the slab and turned them over in her hands. Greta could see the young woman had made her choice.

'Ngghuurr, God.' Erica, startled, looked down to where the noise had come from. Roger was waking up.

Chapter 33

Erica and Roger, side by side, entered the British Museum's Great Court. She stopped for a second in the middle of it to look around. To take a second to reflect on recent events. Everything seemed to be normal. Just another Wednesday. People were wondering around, kids were running, museum invigilators with their big smiles were helping lost tourists. *Perhaps for them nothing changed. The world is still as it was just few days ago*, she thought.

'Erica, are you coming?' asked Roger who was already halfway up the marble staircase.

'Yes, yes, I am.' She quickly joined him. From here, Roger looked different. Maybe it was the light from the great dome above them.

They glanced into each other's eyes and smiled a little shyly. It crossed Erica's mind how funny life could be. It was only last Wednesday that she'd had crush on Bjørn and hoped he would be The One. And now, exactly one week later, she was looking at Roger and thinking, maybe this time… maybe he's the one. She was just about to say something, when a familiar person coming down the stairs interrupted them.

'Professor! Dr Skyberg!' Tony greeted them with a big smile. He looked at his watch a bit surprised. 'I didn't expect you here for another hour!'

'Yes,' said Roger. 'We came to have lunch beforehand. If you'll excuse us,' he pulled Erica's hand as if they were suddenly in a hurry.

She took two steps up, turned around and asked with concern in her voice, 'How is Annabel, Tony?'

Tony paused. 'I don't know, to be honest. I know she is my sister, but I think I just need time, you know, Doctor? I don't know when the trial is set. It's only been three days since her arrest,' he answered, losing his cheerful voice.

'But I just want to make sure that I will be open minded. Not seeing her as murderer or a victim. Just hear her story and try to understand.'

'I see.'

'And what about your gran?'

'Hmmm… It's complicated,' said Erica sadly.

Tony looked at her and said, 'Right then. I'll catch you guys later.' He hurried down the stairs and disappeared among the crowd.

Erica turned around back again and in silence went after Roger to the restaurant on the museum's top floor. They followed a smiley waitress to their table. Erica sat down on the sofa backwards to the window overlooking the Great Court. Roger in front of her.

'Drink?' he asked as soon as they sat down.

'Yeah. I think we do have a reason to celebrate.' Erica smiled at him, and although it was a happy smile, there was more to it.

Roger placed the order and said, 'Listen, I never had a chance to ask why you did it? Why you gave those rings to your grandmother?'

Erica looked up at him and said, 'I don't know if you will be able to understand, but I have never experienced love. So, I don't really know what I gave up. I have lived over thirty years like this, so I think I got used to it. But Gran? She already loves someone. And not just loves someone, but someone loves her back. Me? With or without the curse, I might never meet anyone,' she finished and smiled shyly. Luckily for her in that exact moment, the waitress brought two glasses of champagne.

'Listen, Erica. I-I just wanted to say that everything that happened with your–'

'Granny?' Erica startled, looked down at her phone.

'Yeah, with your granny and everything—'

'No, Roger. My gran is video calling me. Sorry, one second.' She answered her phone. 'Hello?'

'Erica, honey. I was hoping I could still catch you before the press conference. Am I interrupting something?' Erica held her phone out in a way that Greta could see the champagne and Roger. The curator sighed.

'No, of course not, Mrs Skyberg. How can we help you?' he asked, looking with slight fear at her walking stick lying next to her where she sat. He gave Erica a look which said *I hope you won't turn into your gran.*

'I just wanted to thank you again, my dear. Thanks to Detective O'Sullivan I arrived at Svalbard's medical centre right on time. I am pleased to inform, that the antidote seems to be working well.' Relief on her face was easily spotted even among her wrinkles. 'The detective will bring me back to the UK the day after tomorrow, I believe, so I won't disturb the two of you anymore. Bye, bye now.' She sent a virtual kiss and hung up.

Greta looked so happy that Erica knew she would never regret her decision. Love starts with family, after all.

Erica and Roger turned to each other, their eyes locked. They raised their champagne glasses, and both silently hoped that in some magical way, the curse would be lifted anyway. That there was some chance for them.

'Day after tomorrow?' Roger said.

'She paid Tony's sister Annabel to rob a museum,' Erica answered. 'She's as they say *helping Scotland Yard with their inquiries*.'

'Erica, she's your grandmother,' Roger said.

'Yes, she is,' said Erica.

After finished lunch the two curators made their way back to the Great Court.

On the marble staircase Chairman Applegate was talking to the press. He introduced Professor Wright who took a step forward and said:

'Welcome. Thank you. I'm sure you know by now from Scotland Yard, the culprit in the death of Mike Black has been detained, and we have caught the persons responsible for the recent robbery. With great pleasure, on this beautiful Wednesday afternoon, and as the great grandson of the Sir Roger Wright, I am delighted to announced that we have also retrieved the stolen ring and discovered the real Einarr's treasure.'

A flurry of questions came from the reporters including: Will it be displayed here at the British Museum? How did you do it? What was the motive behind the robbery?

Roger answered them as best he could, ending on: 'This wouldn't be possible without help of Dr Erica Skyberg from the Oslo Vikings Museum. We are hoping that she will extend her stay and help us to catalogue the objects found in the tomb. As I said to your question, we would like joint ownership between the two museums of London and Oslo.'

Erica Skyberg watched Roger Wright as he chatted to the press and talked about joint partnerships between the cities and in that moment only one thing came to mind: *I like Wednesdays*, she thought. *They will never be the same.*

The End